Heather's Journey

K.C. Foster

Heather's Journey: Historical Romance of 1930
by K. C. Foster
2nd edition
Copyright © 2024, 2025

ISBN: 979-8-9993695-1-2

Edited by Jeannine Thibodeau *via Reedsy*
Cover art by Sabina Kencana via *Fiverr*

This is a work of fiction. Although the story aligns with an actual historical period, names, characters, some places, and some events are products of the author's imagination. Any resemblance to actual persons, places, or situations is purely coincidental.

Printed in the United States of America

Dedicated to my children

Heather's Journey

Historical Romance of 1930

by

K.C. Foster

Table of Contents

1

Heather in the Dark

eather heard stabbing and creaking outside her house at three o'clock on a fall morning. In her weary awakening, it sounded like rushing water pushed out of a bucket and splashed on the ground, or maybe a door rushed opened with a creak -- no, it was outside. It was with a fury. Maybe an animal was in the garden just behind the house, but with too much passion about something. A creak screamed. It tensed Heather's ears. She lay in bed in the dark, hearing the repetitive stab and creak, stab and creak. In a subconscious sleep, she waited. Then, *stab, creak!* . . . *stab, creak!* Her eyes opened, and she stared at the darkness. What was that? *Who* was that? She got up; her bare feet stiffened with each step across the cold wooden floor. She avoided the spots of the floor that groaned when stepped on; her sister Mae was still asleep.

Stab, creak! . . . *Stab, creak!* She hesitated before getting closer to the back window.

Another step.

Her nose touched the cold pane. The crops were still sleeping, all upright. The dried mounds and trenches were the same. The air was still and dark. Peaceful looking, she thought, until the corner of her left eye saw black shadows move, and light swayed next door in the Whitneys' backyard. The shadows moved softly in one place.

What is that? Heather wondered. She didn't hide; she didn't wake up her father Hugh. She didn't make any distance from her ignorance on darkness. She stepped outside the back door to see more. The cold air rubbed and intruded against her warm cheeks. She felt it revive her senses, and she realized her curiosity would again be frowned upon. But she saw clearly.

Standing behind the Whitney's house, beside their veranda, Old Man Whitney and Renato dug with shovels around a small area, the size of a grave. They stood over a mound of dirt. The stab of their shovels split and dipped in the unbroken earth, and they pushed down their creaking handles. *Stab, creak!* Mrs. Whitney stood with a lantern as she shuffled leaves and yard debris with her feet over the fresh earth.

Heather was seeing something she wasn't supposed to. She froze in place, afraid to move, afraid they'd see her. They didn't see her for a time. When they did, she offered an innocent good morning. They paused and stared at her. Mrs. Whitney returned the greeting. As Old Man Whitney continued his digging, Renato stood still with his shovel for a moment before ambling towards Heather through the grass, using his shovel like a cane.

As he came nearer, Heather saw more clearly his disarrayed hair, and how it crowned his troubled, dirty face. Dirt spots smudged on his arms, his rolled-up sleeves, and his clothes. His eyes stared at Heather sadly, wearily. His face was shiny with sweat and glistened in the night sky. His breath was deep. Something bothered him, Heather could tell. But she admired his passion in the distress.

"Ren, you okay? You wanna come in? What are you doing?"

"Come in, Ren," Hugh's voice boomed from behind and startled Heather. "Let's have some coffee."

Heather placed a kettle on the stove while Renato washed his hands and face. Renato and Hugh sat at the kitchen table leaning on their forearms. Heather lit a lantern for soft light. They had electrical power; everyone in Sterling, Illinois, did — thanks to the Whitneys, but the lantern still had a place in everyone's lives in 1930.

The three of them kept subdued, partly because Mae still slept.

"I didn't kill anybody, Hugh, in case you're wondering," Renato said as he leaned back in his chair, "and I didn't see — whoever the man is in the ground — I wasn't around. I was still awake when Old Man Whitney pulled in his driveway. I walked over, and . . . he's old. He needed my help. That's all." Renato shook his head. "They're old, Hugh. They're not bad people. You don't think so, do you? I don't think Mr. Whitney killed nobody neither," Renato slowly leaned forward in his chair. "He said he was helping out someone. Probably trying to do good. Don't you think?" He said all he could say. Heather strained the coffee grounds in a pot as the steam from the kettle lifted to the ceiling. From the pot, she dipped Hugh and Renato some coffee.

"No, you're right. They're good people," Hugh said, sitting calmly with an arm resting on the table. "You're devoted and loyal, Renato, and more than me. Much more. 'Cause I heard him, too, coming home, and I rolled back over to sleep. You know why? 'Cause I don't want no part of ending a man's life," Hugh spoke with an admirable soft confidence. "That's where I gotta draw the line, see." They sat still and quiet as Hugh stared at Renato. Finally, Hugh asked, "Did you help bury him?"

"Yeah," Renato's voice cracked, cupping his coffee mug, staring at it. Small pause.

"There's honor in that," Hugh said, nodding his head. More silence for a few more minutes, they stared solemnly in space and sipped their coffee. Heather poured the leftover coffee in a cup for herself and joined them at the table. The men welcomed her with cordial smiles that broke the tension.

Renato soon stood to leave for his home across the street, to wash up and get ready for work.

"Thanks for the coffee, Heather," Renato said, and he left.

And everyone went on about their morning. No need to regain composure; none was yet lost.

2

The Renato

R enato Reyes-Sanchez was Illinois' swoon and reason for giggling amidst the Great Depression. A scatter-full of girls felt prettier if they were regarded by Renato. They acted as if he enraptured them with just his eyes. No wink, no romantic gestures, not even a smile. Just a soft stare the girls loved. Not an intentional look; he just didn't know what to say or what to do or how to act. So, he stared. Renato never initiated nor instigated being noticed to lead poor dames to his lair. A charmer innately, with his rebel traces of shiny black, slicked-back hair falling on his forehead. His neck often slumped forward, causing him to lower his head. It made him look like he did something wrong, or like he had no confidence in himself. Maybe girls resorted to thinking they were who— or what —he needed. Also hard to overlook were his hands. He regularly kept cracks on his knuckles. Occasionally, he'd have a busted lip or a swell somewhere on his face, typically from a Chicago speakeasy he, Hugh, and Old Man Whitney rolled in. After each bloody face, ladies doted around Renato to clean up blood, give him a drink and a kiss. Hugh and Old Man Whitney stormed their anger on Renato every time he fought.

"Can we not go have a good time without getting shot?" Hugh screamed. "You're gonna get us shot with that mouth of yours!"

No matter. The girls were drawn to the bad boy.

Renato and Heather worked for Hugh at Dodge Grocers, and some mornings Renato kept his sleeves down and buttoned. Just before Renato engaged in something he found to be important, he unbuttoned his cuffs and rolled up his sleeves, whether he plowed dirt, cooked a Puerto Rican dish, or wrote a letter to his mother. If sleeves remained down, he proceeded with little effort, like when he stocked the shelves or helped customers. Most of the time, sleeves were down. even as a degradation of lady-like poise strutted in the store on a daily basis. Take Lilac Blanton, for example. They expected her to come in the store almost daily; and on most days, this twenty-something year old bought nothing more than candy. She was a Sterling farmer's daughter.

"Here comes Lilac," Hugh said, peering out the store's front door.

"Again?" Heather complained. "The girl obviously can't tell when she acts like a fool!"

"Shut up and be nice," Hugh strained out as Lilac came closer to the door.

"God, look at her," Heather looked from a front window.

"A profusion of awkward!"

"Girl, what's wrong with you! What did you say?" Hugh glared at Heather before the door rang open.

Lilac waddled in, looked around, and stood at the counter. She gave a fake smile that set uncomfortably on her frail face. Heather was compelled to keep her distance. Lilac's blond, fine hair looked as if she did nothing more than rub it down with her hands.

"Daddy just wonderin' if the grain sold yet," her twangy soft voice was directed towards Hugh.

"Not yet, ma'am. He just brought it in two days ago," Hugh answered Lilac sternly as he stood behind the counter, still perturbed with Heather. But Lilac asked the same question yesterday. Lilac chuckled and shifted her feet like she wished she had something else to say.

Sometimes, she did: "I didn't go to work today. Daddy needed help with the corn," and "I missed work today, helping our sick neighbors," and "I was feeling ill this morning, so I just woke up. I'm better now." Heather didn't believe anything she said, and she insisted Hugh and Renato didn't either.

On this day, Renato stared at Lilac, leaned his elbows on the counter by the register, and said, "Lilac, you want some scotch? Unless you need to get back to the farm, . . . or go to work, . . . or-"

Shame on him! thought Heather. *Teasing her lack of flirting skills.* No one else was in the store, and they had a weakness for interpreting downtime as playtime.

"I'll have some," Heather wryly intervened.

"Shut up, Heather," Renato mumbled out as he poured

Lilac a shot.

Lilac stared at Renato, which meant *Yes, pour me a shot,* without having to admit it. She took the tin cup slowly as if she wondered if Renato was leading her into temptation.

"You don't have to drink that, Lilac," Heather tried again and placed her inventory notebook on the counter. Hugh didn't intervene; he looked curiously entertained. With Heather's insult of petting, Lilac gulped the scotch like water, followed with a strain in her stiffened neck like she was being strangled. Redness covered her face with a cacophony from her throat – deep coughs followed by moans and grunts. An ugly conglomeration of sights and sounds! Once regaining her composure, she stared at Renato with wide eyes and laughed. She never helped on the farm that day, but she felt pretty.

Renato and Hugh both grew up in Savannah, Georgia, although many years apart in age. The northern part of Sterling, Illinois, was Renato's stopping and turn-around place for bootlegging trips made to Chicago and Pittsburgh. A pitstop like Sterling became an extended hibernating point for Renato. Hugh needed Renato to help work at the store as a White man— almost white. Renato was Puerto Rican, which was on the white side. Also, since he was handsome and good with the ladies, he was good for whatever business they could get. Hugh was threatened to be closed down on a regular basis due to "a colored man being in charge of putting food on Sterling's tables." But Renato's side job of tonic satisfaction wooed the townsfolk silent, except the ones he fought with.

Renato got kicked out of the Savannah schools when he

was younger. Life experiences took precedence over school persuasions for Renato as a boy, and he knew the business of rum running and bootlegging. The Reyes-Sanchez family placed some Puerto-Rican roots among the ports of Brunswick, Georgia, just south of Savannah. Their "Papa" worked cargo quality and safety. That was their formal way of saying rum running and bootlegging — "cargo quality and safety." Hugh occasionally gave his rebuke of Renato's bootlegging while holding a glass of scotch in his own hand.

"The business is illegal, and illegal is wrong," Hugh would fuss, "and if it's not wrong, it leads you the wrong way."

Renato rarely argued or debated with Hugh over the subject. He regarded Hugh as his best friend, and Hugh daily offered Renato a wealth of fatherly advice. But rebellion trails behind, like it has to, like the aroma of a drinker -- a stench to one and a fragrance to another, however one may deem the smell. It depends on the rebel.

3

The Malady of Mae

The incident of body-burying wasn't brought up again, except by 12-year-old Mae.

"Why's it all dug up right here, Mrs. Whitney?" Mae's voice blared one afternoon, standing in the Whitneys' back yard.

"Mind your own business, Mae! And don't be so nosy!" Mrs. Whitney snapped.

"Well," Mae continued, "if you'd answer my question, I wouldn't be nosy anymore."

"It's just yard work, Mae," Mrs. Whitney lied. "Yard work often involves digging, now, don't it?"

Mae spent much of her time at the Whitneys' grand antebellum-style home. Mae believed she had special privileges as a next-door neighbor, and as a healthy-sized girl, and as a brown girl, and as a singer's daughter, and as an admired human who had yet embraced the concept of boundaries.

The same with Renato, and together they created

unnerving, hysterical bedlam.

Renato visited the Randolph home almost daily, showing up with his suspenders pulled off. He'd let them hang on his sides from his hips.

"You ain't afraid of your pants falling down, Renato?" Mae once asked. Everyone was congregated in the kitchen, delegating chores for dinner. All but Mae. As Renato larded a skillet with rolled sleeves, Mae did nothing but stare in a hand mirror at her large curls and how they rounded her chubby head which sat atop of her chubby shoulders protruding out her chubby brown arms.

Renato paused from his work, pierced serious eyes at Mae, and told her, "You better not touch 'em. I'll smack you."

Mae said nothing, but she must have conjured a plan with polished time; as he stood over the coal burner with hands occupied, she lunged toward him and quickly swiped down his pants with her two chubby hand grips. Heather gasped, Renato hollered, "Mae!" and Mae laughed loud and hard.

Renato's bare legs stood exposed. His shirt fell with just enough depth to cover everything above the curves of his butt cheeks. Renato turned around to pull his pants up quickly. He didn't smile. Hugh took Mae to his bedroom for a whipping, and his angry voice boomed and vibrated the walls. Renato and Heather heard the first "WOP!", and things were quiet for a small second before they heard Mae roll into more laughter. Hugh hollered some more and another "WOP!" Things were quiet other than Hugh's anger. Hugh didn't whip her anymore. Renato pulled his suspenders back over his shoulders, for that day, at least.

"You better think about keeping those suspenders up. I

ain't scared to pull down your pants again," Mae said as she waltzed in the kitchen.

No one ever stayed angry with Mae, and she took advantage of this gift.

The next morning at Dodge Grocers, the doorbell rang, and Mae walked in the door.

"What the hell!" shouted Hugh.

Mae proudly held a dead limp duck around the neck with one hand and hugged its lifeless body in her other arm. Heather held out on having a smoke to see this. After Hugh's shout, Mae stopped in the middle of the store. She managed to keep looped, jovial curls around her head. She slept with a nightcap covering the night before, and each curl was still intact. She stood with her shoulders back, and she could look loud without saying a thing.

"Mrs. Whitney told me I should pluck this duck. Daddy, I can't! I don't know how! And this poor dead bird makes me sad, . . ." She hugged it closer to her and turned side to side with her feet planted.

"Mae, you look like an idiot," Heather said.

"Get that dead animal out of my store, Mae! Now!"

"Are you gonna pluck it?"

"I'll start some hot water," Renato offered. He refilled the kettle with water and placed it on the stove.

"Mae, out!" Hugh raised his voice.

"I'll pluck it, Mae. Hold on," Renato chimed in. "Hot water will help the feathers fall out."

"Mae, out!" Hugh roared.

"Alright, Hugh, we're leaving," Renato rushed around the

counter. "Will you still hug on Mr. Quack-Quack when he ain't got feathers?" Renato kept walking towards the door.

"Mae, out!" Hugh repeated, pointing his finger at the door and stomping towards Mae. Hugh swayed his arms in anger, knocking a display of balms off the counter.

Mae stood defying her daddy, holding that bird in the middle of the store. She said, "I don't hug naked birds!" Mae ran out behind Renato before Hugh reached her. She was in the center of a stage wherever she went.

Once the plucking was done, Renato started towards the back to the store office. "Take a letter to the post office, Mae," Renato said. Renato faithfully wrote letters to his mother in Savannah. He handed Mae the letter.

"I'm gonna write my Momma, too," Mae proclaimed.

Renato looked baffled and said, "I got some letters for your Ma, Mae. Four of 'em, followed by the word *you*," Renato looked at Hugh, pleased with his wit.

"Why do you write your momma all the time?" Mae asked, watching him unpack a box of cans.

"Don't worry about it," Renato answered, but Mae stared. "So she don't worry, that's why. She's Boricua." Hugh nodded his head with a couple of "Yups" in agreement from behind the counter, eyeing Mae.

"If I don't write, she'll get mean," Renato said, "like your Ma."

"My momma's not mean!" Mae peered with slanted eyes at Renato and hands on her hips, bending the envelope.

"You got the meanest mother alive, wouldn't waste my spit on her," Renato commented.

"Hey, hey," Hugh said in a low voice. "Too far, Renato, that's the girl's mother." Hugh never said an ugly word about his estranged wife, the missing mother of their two girls.

Heather and Mae's mother was Sylvia. She took off — busted out for big-time when Heather was eleven and Mae was seven. Heather had eight years since then to figure out the world. Sylvia showed up to say hello about twice a year, yet not every year, never expectedly, and never on holidays or birthdays. Heather tried not to remember her, but she paid attention to her Momma's stature for comparison when she did come around. Sylvia was flauntingly tall, but her height seemed to vary in all sorts of lengths each time she came back around. Her shoulders were always so broad that the corners of her shoulders pointed out left and right. She pulled her black hair back tight. The girls couldn't tell how long it was. She did have a football oval face and pointy chin. She sang— apparently; her voice pulled her away from Illinois. She said it traveled to the big city, and she had to follow it. She "felt smothered," . . . "suffocated," . . . "couldn't breathe" —her family "kept her from flying." She fluttered for New York to live her dream. In her dream, Heather nor Mae nor Hugh existed. Except sometimes, when she came to visit.

Those were unfortunate days, but they were also the happiest days in Mae's life.

4

Life at Dodge Grocers

*H*eather spent most of her girlhood at Dodge Grocers. The store grounded and soared with the help of a Savannah abolitionist family, the Haversons, and their connections with fellow Illinois abolitionists, the Whitneys and the Dodges. Hugh spoke of the Dodge family with so much admiration; his father named the store after them. Hugh truly thought the store, along with all these good moments, would prosper forever.

The store was alone, a quarter of a mile away from the Main Square. The bare parking area of the store stayed empty more than they liked. The brick square building had a green metal sign glazed dull with dust over bold red letters, "Dodge Grocers," screwed to the front of the building over the double doors. Sun and time depleted its luster. Even the smaller sign in the window, a picture of bread and butter, signifying the Dodge family, was faded and tired out. A wooden table sat

17

on the front porch piled with straw baskets for customers. Hugh often sat in the chair beside the table, almost camouflaged in his gray suit and dark black skin. He knew he was difficult to see when he sat there; he enjoyed seeing startled faces as customers walked closer to the door. Hugh stood to offer a handshake to every guest. He sat out there when he wasn't busy, even if it was too cold to be comfortable.

Back in the warm store, the day's duties commenced. "Henry Grayson wants to place some of his meat in our cooler," Hugh said, leaned against the counter. He, Renato, and Heather were the only three in the store at the time. "His cooler is broken. It's never worked right, and he can't afford to buy a new one right now," he continued as he drank his hot coffee.

"I know, Daddy. He doesn't have a freon compressor," Heather said.

The conversation died as Hugh and Renato sipped their coffee. Heather grabbed a pack of cigarettes and headed towards the door.

A couple of hours passed on at Dodge Grocers. The doorbell sounded, and Heather got used to the disappointment that not only was "Momma" not coming through the door, but the man of her dreams didn't stroll through either. Just another customer, or Hugh, or Renato.

But Heather kept dreaming. She imagined the ding of the door when the golden rays of sun shone through the windows, still early, when her skin looked rich and smooth. There Heather's man would stand at the door, looking around softly, and then he'd shake hands with her father. He'd look around some more and meet Heather's eyes. After that her dream was a blur. Time and time again, just customers. Sometimes, Veronica.

Veronica Nolan was a frequent customer, and an heir to a notable Illinois fortune. She was the only child of the wealthy Nolan couple. Their family tree founded and owned the metal businesses in northern Illinois, with headquarters in Sterling.

The people of Sterling believed France changed Veronica. She left for France just before the war, and just before Sterling's common-folk peacekeepers snapped against the Nolans for allowing the young Veronica to behave shamelessly — revealing cleavage as soon as she had it. She wore even fewer clothes after a trip to the Caribbean. Furthermore, she drank her whiskey publicly, no attempts to hide it as everyone else, as if she was immune to the Prohibition. "Money can truly make one immune to the things that disease the poor," Mrs. Whitney commented. Veronica giggled away with men, even married men. She was beautiful, rich, and could shake a girl's confidence and boost a boy's dream.

Several Americans of wealth and nobility "stationed" themselves overseas just before the war, including the reckless Veronica.

A year later she came home so poised and proper and matured the town wondered if the woman was an imposture. One can tell when a woman walks on a foundation of morals and values, or when there's not one at all. Veronica finally "firmed her ground right," Sterling townsfolk said. Veronica was still rich, beautiful, and confident, but she dressed in plainer clothes, and she stood more rigid, as if one could try to push her and she wouldn't budge. She also rarely turned her head to the right or to the left, as if in fear she may see something to drive her into a panic.

What happened on the other side of the ocean? What did she see? Questions arose with no answers. Her long, blond hair still danced and shined, holding remnants of her past. Veronica was quite a poised beauty.

She'd find Renato in Dodge Grocers and roll out an engaging, long-lasting conversation. Heather viewed her like a vulture with wings extended, swinging her hips and flinging her hair, keeping all other wild animals away from her feast. Veronica had a natural way of owning her territory, giving Heather an inferior feeling in her own family's store. She usually escaped to the back office when Veronica prolonged customer privileges.

"Heather," Hugh came to Heather in the office one day, "what's wrong? You jealous?"

"Daddy! Jealous of what? I'm not throwing myself at Renato like Veronica does. That's all. I'm not jealous of her."

Heather was a thief with no conviction. She stole many items from Dodge Grocers. She pocketed cigarettes, soap, candy, silverware that no one was buying. Anything that would not spoil and that would fit nicely in a suitcase preparing to one day leave for Savannah. She kept inventory at the store, so she knew what an insignificant amount to steal was. She was nineteen and wanted to be a woman elsewhere.

She was nine years old when women were given the right to vote. As a young girl, she walked into Dodge Grocers, and Hugh stood in front of the counter with a grand smile for his girl. Even a hug. Hugh didn't mention how her color might get in the way, but he wanted her to feel free. As encouraging as that day was, Heather had felt a pull towards Savannah since she was much younger. Savannah was where Heather knew she could break away from scruples.

Heather lived under the goodness of a good town and a good Daddy. She loved the wind in Illinois that tried to tell her so many secrets from the west. But she dreamed of being in love in Savannah. She thought about this man in detail; he was basically Black and sweaty. He'd come home sweaty from work in the evening, and his skin would shine brighter than the sun. He'd smile and say, "It's hot outside, Heather." And he'd start singing like an angel every night to her, no matter how hot it was, or how hard he'd been working. She'd wrap her arms around him and get coated with his liquid gold of sweat. They'd be in love. She saw him in her dreams, and she dreamed about him a lot.

One early evening, Heather sat on her bed and stared out the window. The full moon softened the air into a silvery translucence. And there he was. He stood in the middle of the road with the moonlight shining on his black rich skin, thick shoulders and chest. His collar wide around the bottom of his neck, revealing a glimpse of his chest. Breathing steam of manliness like a bull and standing in his moonlit throne, wondering if his Northern Illinois girl was nearby. Then he turned his eyes and caught Heather staring at him through her bedroom window. Her pulse giggled. Then TAP, TAP, TAP!

"Heather! What are you thinking about?" Renato stood outside her window laughing. *Where did he come from? I didn't even see him!* She was flustered after jumping frantically at his tap.

"Get away from Heather's window, Ren!" Hugh hollered at Renato from the front door.

"She's in a dream world in there!" Renato backed up and smiled at Heather. He embarrassed her.

"I'm sorry I startled you," Renato poked his head in Heather's bedroom door.

"Are you?" she bantered as she stood up and walked out of her room.

Heather's dream wasn't just a dream anymore. She knew it as her future, her ticket to getting out of this fenced-in playground; the steps to womanhood; and as long as she stayed still, she wasn't going to it.

5

And The Whitneys

Old Man Whitney was murdered. Renato wrote a letter home to his mother in Savannah and said so.

"Heather, help me write, okay?" He valued Heather's opinion on his finished letters. They sat at the store's back-office table. Things were quiet as Hugh watched the store floor. The office was small with a back door and a window that gave a dull light to the brown-walled room, half-organized with cans, bottles, and cardboard boxes. The dull room understood the mood. Old Man Whitney was gone. Renato's sleeves were already rolled up, and he began to read what he'd written:

"Hola Ma, Old Man Whitney was shot dead."

Mr. and Mrs. Whitney had a wealth of connections from Savannah, Georgia, to Chicago, Illinois. Along with being active abolitionists, they were investors in the illegal distribution and sales of alcohol. The Whitney couple were the ones who invited Renato to take a break and live in Sterling, away from the rising dangers of bootlegging. They gave him a home across the street from their own. Renato himself knew the bootlegging business and made several connections.

The Whitneys were where needs were met, when they were needed by countless debtors. They helped people. They helped the town purchase its first 35-horsepower tractor with a moldboard plow. They helped harvest the corn without asking for a single ear. All town meetings ended with whatever solutions the Whitneys offered. They owned the Randolph house. Unmatched in ingenuity were the Whitneys. They always got their way, and they were undoubtedly respected.

"He will be buried in the morning quickly -- the summer heat's no good for a dead body above ground for too long, as you probably know.

"Ma, I didn't kill him. I had nothing to do with it. I promise. He was my friend.

"Illinois is good, but I miss you and you know I love you. No worries, but I'm staying a while longer. Then I'll be home."

His last four words startled Heather; Renato didn't consider Illinois his home? She wasn't sure she could mask the insult, like he was infringing upon a mutuality that he had no right to redefine.

"You're not home?" Heather asked and stared at him.

"Yeah, I'm home, Heather, but not at my first home, and not how Ma sees it," he answered. "If she heard me call anywhere other than where she's at home, it would break Ma's heart."

"Was she sad when you left?"

"Nah, as long as I know where home is."

"Home is Savannah?"

"Yeah, Heather. Stupid question." Renato nodded and studied his letter. He stopped and looked at Heather with surprise.

"Do I break your heart, Heather?" He asked and stared at Heather.

Heather tried to keep her eyes from shifting and answered, "No, it's just a sad day. Poor Mrs. Whitney. Alone. Husband gone suddenly. I'll miss him, too. I can't believe he's gone."

"Sí, but it's life, Heather," Renato said, "When two people are in love, they know they're risking either seeing one die or dying. It's life. No surprises." Renato stared at Heather as he folded up his letter and placed it in an envelope.

Heather replied, "I like surprises. And love is worth it."

"I agree," Renato said, looking away.

Heather stared and tapped her fingers on the table before asking, "Do you know who shot Old Man Whitney?"

Renato's eyes opened wide towards her. "No, Heather. I was nowhere around. Mrs. Whitney got a call. He was found dead. Shot." Renato stood up to walk out. "You know, I loved him, too, Heather."

The funeral was in the Whitneys' home. Many men in suits and an equal number of men in overalls filled the home. The Nolan family and the Haversons were there, too.

Looking for a familiar face, Heather asked her father, "Where's Ren?"

"Don't bother lookin for him. He ain't here."

6

Bruises Turn Blue

The merry bell rang at the opening of the store's door, and misled Heather and Hugh to expect a smile at its announcement. With no smile, Renato walked in with a purple swollen eye and a cut lip with a mixture of flesh and dried blood. His eyes moved like they were trapped behind a beaten mask. Heather and Hugh paused their morning work and stared for a moment. Heather gasped in shock.

"Ren, go back home," Hugh said in a low deep voice, standing behind the register.

"Hugh," Renato began and stopped on the other side of the counter. He looked around the store and back at Hugh. "Can we talk?" No one else was in the store.

"You okay, Ren?" Heather offered and walked up beside him. Renato nodded at her and pierced his eyes towards her with sagacity.

They resettled at the back corner of the store where the warm stove covered heat over a couch and two wooden chairs. Hugh poured Renato a cup of coffee. Heather sat beside Hugh, across from Renato. The air was still heavy with remnants of Old Man Whitney's funeral just the day before. Few customers had entered the store on this late morning.

"Hugh, I know who Old Man Whitney and I buried — well, I know why he buried the man. I don't actually know who he was," Renato strained out and sipped his coffee.

"Okay," Hugh answered, "why'd he bury him?"

Renato hesitated and rolled words around in his mouth before speaking. "He made a deal with one of the guys in Pittsburgh . . . that owns the strip. . . to never book Sylvia."

"Sylvia?" Hugh straightened up in his chair and deepened his eyebrows towards Renato.

"Yeah, Old Man Whitney had her banned from performing on the strip. I don't know why. I just know . . ." Renato looked up to find his words, "he said he didn't like seeing how she mistreated you and the girls."

"Okay," Hugh turned his head to the side and gave an irritable huff and said, "so he had her banned." Hugh shifted in his seat and asked, "Why'd Old Man Whitney bury a man in his back yard?"

"Part of the deal to not book Sylvia. Bury evidence. A body." Everyone sat quietly for a while. There was more to be revealed, but Hugh and Heather engaged in appreciating the silence and ignorance.

"Ren," Hugh stared and his voice saddened, "why are you beat up?"

"I went looking for Old Man's killer," Renato answered and looked down. "He'd done the same for me, Hugh. And you."

"We got police officers, don't we? Then maybe there

wouldn't be so many killings, you see, Ren? Can't you see that?"

"Come on, police ain't helping," Renato answered.

"Neither are you!" Neither is Old Man Whitney!" Hugh stood up and stared down at Renato. "Did you find the killer?"

"No. But I know, Hugh — and you're not gonna believe me — it's somebody that knows Sylvia."

"Ren, stop!"

"About five guys, Hugh — her friends, jumped on me last night, Hugh."

Heather joined in, "Wait, Ren, you're telling me Momma had something to do with Old Man Whitney's murder?"

As Renato answered "yes," Hugh answered, "Your mother didn't kill anybody, Heather! Don't listen to him!"

"The same guys who probably jumped on Old Man Whitney, except I didn't get shot."

"How do you know that?" Heather asked.

"Enough!" Hugh's voice roared in anger. "Go home, Ren."

As Renato walked out of the store, Hugh turned to Heather, "Your mother's not like that, Heather. Ren just don't like her. And I guess Old Man Whitney didn't care for her either. She did things differently, that's all. She's still your mother. Don't listen to Ren."

Days began to cool, and people started moving slower. Not as many places to go anymore. The store was able to keep its doors open. A few local gardens and farms were failing, and the store gave the Sterling people a buffer. Relief. Days turned from orange to brown with crisp air, and crunchy leaves blanketed roads and sidewalks.

No one brought up Old Man Whitney's murder again.

7

Shots from a Flower

A bit northward in Illinois, winter could be felt from afar, like ghosts floating slowly to dampen Illinois. Heather felt alone and free when she walked to the store. Alone and free, she lit a cigarette. It gave her an older look, she was certain, and townspeople often didn't see her as a woman making her own decisions. Maybe they did, but she was tired of hearing how she was "just a little girl yesterday" as she puffed her cigarette, always asking for Hugh when they came in the store, and then proud of Heather for proving competency, enthralled with the development of time.

She loved Illinois. The Depression was awakening and rising around the Randolph's. Grown-up farms with deep eroded pits, abandoned homes and barns, hollowed out cars being pulled by a donkey or a tired horse — it was all so burdening to one's eyes that the air loomed brown. Businesses were left bare, with "Closed" signs hanging on the doors. Those affected the most showed it on their faces, like misery. Everyone's affection for one another resorted to greater love or fatal hate. Nevertheless, townsfolk knew Illinois, its character, stuff that other people from other places couldn't see, like knowing a family member. There was a grassy spot north of Sterling where locust trees and crab apple trees were scattered, dividing the community from the interminable expanse of farms. Everyone had some type of memory there.

Heather passed through the square without pausing to be cordial to anyone. The only way to battle the frigid wind was to walk quickly all the way to Dodge Grocers. Upon entering the store, Hugh and Renato were engaged in a conversation, giving Heather's entry little notice.

"Did you write the family back?" Hugh asked. The warmth of the store soothed the coldness of the conversation.

"Not yet." Renato sat on a stool at the back of store as Hugh stood across from him.

"Keeping the folks waiting? What's your plans?" Hugh sounded like a father.

"I . . . I guess I'll go." The warm interior now couldn't relax the tension. Heather's spirit plummeted.

Renato is leaving us? Heather wondered. The time had come for changes, but Heather wanted to go back to yesterday.

"Okay, . . . good. You need to," Hugh answered. Hugh spoke as a good mentor, but Heather wondered if his heart was breaking as hers was. Hugh dumped another small heap of coal into the burner. "But, Renato, how am I gonna take care of these crazy girls without you?" Hugh winked at Heather, but she was insulted.

"Daddy, I take care of you," Heather retorted.

An intention of comic relief, but Hugh didn't smile. Renato tried.

"You gotta go to Mama Rey," Hugh added, staring at Renato with a relaxed expression. Heather believed her Daddy cared nothing about his own emotions, ever. He wanted everyone else to be happy, even Sylvia, and now he wanted to appease Renato.

"Yeah. . .Yeah, of course. I'm always excited to see Ma," Renato replied, staring at his rearrangement of food cans on the display table.

"Well," started Hugh, "it doesn't sound like they're asking you to come down and *see* them. They're not asking for a visit. You see that, right?"

"Yeah, Hugh. Hell, I know, I know," Renato snapped.

Heather found his response puzzling. Did he feel guilty? *Momma never felt guilty about leaving.* Heather thought. She was preparing to leave herself. At some point, everyone leaves home, but Heather didn't know the right way versus the wrong way. She dreamed daily of leaving for Savannah, leaving Hugh, and leaving Mae. But reality happened now. Perhaps a purposeful new reality was ready for her now.

"I'll miss you," Heather offered, "Unless you take me with you?" She made her words sound like a frivolous gesture. Renato didn't smile, but he looked at Hugh with a curious stare. Hugh fixed his face to be blank of any expression.

"Renato, . . ." Heather began.

The store door opened and a man frantically swooped in. His over-sized wool blazer swallowed his slim frame. His fedora covered a mess of hair. He scoped the store with big round eyes, shifting them quickly under angry eyebrows. Heather backed up and stood in the opposite back corner. She saw a rusty car, an older T Model, still running outside the door. A pop of color bled through the windshield of the car, material with red splatter with blue in the middle. A flower?

"Hey, Mister – what's your hurry today?" Hugh took his post behind the cooler, "How can I-"

"Don't help me!" shouted the stranger, "Don't help me!" The man looked at Renato. "Is this Hugh Randolph?"

Heather's chest felt hot. She felt her pulse in the front of her face beating. Hugh glanced over at her, and back at the customer. Heather stepped quietly behind the shelves of food. She was a little girl again.

"Sir, . . . yes sir. I'm Hugh Randolph. I own this store. Can I help you?"

The man pulled out a gun and pointed it at Hugh. Heather's heart pounded from her chest to her throat to her entire head. Her head pulsed, and she breathed harder in hopes she wouldn't pass out.

"Don't shoot," Hugh threw up his hands. "Mister, have mercy. I got two girls-"

"Open the drawer and give me the money," the man growled with his teeth grinding together. The cash register rang merrily. Heather counted the money last night; there was $12.00 in there along with a few coins. She couldn't hear the man's orders anymore, and things became a blur. She noticed a stream of light from the sun that made a diagonal tunnel through the air of the store. The man was grabbing everything that was in arm's reach and throwing the things into a burlap bag in Hugh's hands. Heather heard Renato's voice say "Heather," but she couldn't comprehend anything else. The door stayed closed. The car outside kept chuckling. No one else came in. Heather heard Daddy's voice. He stood tall. Distinguished. The red and blue flower on the silk-looking material relaxed over the seat of the car.

Renato shouted for the man to leave and threw cans at him with a thrust of force. A surge of anger erupted from Heather's chest. Each tin can flew too slowly to its target, despite the force Renato shoved behind each one. The man pointed the gun at Renato and shot through the line of cans. Renato's legs turned weak, and he fell to his side. A stream of red soaked a spot on the side of his shirt. Heather was frantic and crying, feeling dizzy.

"Go!" Heather's voice muffled out to no more than a whisper with all the strength it could. Hugh's eyes pierced sternly at Heather and then at the robber.

The man turned to stare at Hugh. "Just doing my job, Hugh Randolph!" the man gritted and fired the gun at Hugh. Hugh fell behind the counter and out of sight.

Heather heard the gun shoot again. Her breaths shortened. A red painted flower with a blue speck in the middle clouded her vision. Then everything turned black.

8

Dusk

eather hardly opened her eyes, and distress blanketed over her. It seeped through her skin, through her head, and ached in her chest. Her head pounded. Her vision was blurry. *Something bad happened.* That's all she knew for sure for quite a few minutes. She lay in bed motionless and closed her eyes. She heard a rattling sound, and a thug of a cup being set on her bedside table. The sounds tensed the pain in her head. Her eyes opened again, and Mrs. Whitney sat in a chair beside her. Mrs. Whitney focused on the side of the bed, with her hand cupped around a glass set on Heather's nightstand. She perked when she noticed Heather was awake.

"I don't know why I take these yeast pills, . . . vitamins. Or something," Mrs. Whitney's voice cracked as she spoke as if Heather was interrogating her, demanding answers. Heather kept her head on the pillow, resting her gaze on Mrs. Whitney. She was afraid to move her aching head. Nausea swelled.

"They're supposed to make me feel better, but . . . I don't see the point of hopeless people taking anything for improvement," Mrs. Whitney forced out a sad chuckle. Heather and Mrs. Whitney remained still for another moment, both of them with long faces, but Heather was still not sure why.

"I'm happy you're awake, Heather," Mrs. Whitney attempted to soothe Heather with her cracked strain. She was holding back a cry.

A dullness jumped right in front of Mrs. Whitney's words. She stared at Heather while they heard Mae's voice, weeping.

"Mae?" Heather sat up quickly, causing dizziness and nausea. Mrs. Whitney cradled Heather around the shoulders.

"You passed out and hit your head at the store," Mrs. Whitney managed as she whimpered. Heather stared at her for more information, "Heather, your daddy passed away today." Mrs. Whitney rubbed her arm and grabbed her hand. Her face wrinkled helplessly with a full cry.

Heather dry-heaved sitting in the bed. Mrs. Whitney held her. Despite her weakness, she stumbled to find Mae in the living room, and the air, the walls, the floor, and the ceiling all felt different without the presence of their Daddy. Mae buried her wet swollen face in Heather's chest. Heather looked around for her Daddy, not believing he could be gone. She panted and waited for the nausea and dizziness to leave her.

"Mae, where's Renato?" Heather asked.

"He won't wake up," Mae cried out.

"We're praying he'll recover, Heather," Mrs. Whitney sat on the edge of the couch, giving Mae and Heather some distance. Together, they sat in the dark. Heather couldn't breathe. She gasped and stumbled out the back door to wail out her grief. Her head felt bruised and throbbed. The three of them submitted to the mourning for the remainder of the long, brutal day, feeling in limbo between still feeling the existence of Hugh and being sucked into time that kept walking past them, further away from their Daddy.

Please! Don't take Daddy! Time is apathetic when a Daddy dies, and it wouldn't stop for Heather.

Renato was still unconscious on the day of Hugh's funeral. Many people from Sterling attended, even some white people. Many of the same faces from Old Man Whitney's funeral were there. Men in fedoras and dark suits and black trench coats multiplied with the colored people forming a scatter of pepper. Hugh was respected. He conducted business with local farmers, selling local crops in his store, making connections and staying up to date with Hoover's latest poke for hope. Sterling knew Hugh, and many of them knew Heather. Many asked and scoffed if Heather was the new owner of Dodge Grocers. Sounded dreadful to Heather as she was sure it did to many Sterling residents. She had no plans for days to come. She didn't care.

Why was Daddy gone? Who killed him? Was he caught? Arrested? Why did he shoot Daddy?

Heather had planned to leave her father, but she never wanted him to leave her. She didn't receive any answers concerning the murderer. Mrs. Whitney confidently repeated that finding the murderer would be an easy task. Heather believed her.

"You don't think Momma was connected in any way, do

you, Mrs. Whitney?"

Mrs. Whitney sat tall and pursed her lips, staring at Heather as if disappointed with her statement. "I won't accuse your mother of such, but I promised your daddy I'd never speak ill of your mother to you nor in front of you. So change the subject, Heather."

Mrs. Whitney's spark as an abolitionist dimly burned with brittle old legs now. Old Man Whitney, her partner in rigor, was gone. Her face looked longer. Her hair was brittle and not as coiffure-like as usual. Her overall demeanor was gray. But when she spoke to Heather about finding Daddy's killer, Heather saw the spunky, colorful Mrs. Whitney again. She loved Mae and Heather, and it kept her tenacious, despite her progressing hopelessness.

9

Momma

Mae and Heather visited Renato every day. He had been shot in the side, and he still lay asleep, not conscious yet. Heather partnered with Mrs. Whitney and the doctor to help Renato heal, checking for fever and swells. This task relieved Heather of gloom. She tried not to glance out Renato's windows to see her own home, where her Daddy wasn't. She imagined Hugh would be sitting right where she was, tending to Renato himself. The doctor came by every day to give Renato fluids. When no one else was at his home, Heather sat by Renato's bed and stared at him. She had never had the freedom to stare and study his face without him knowing.

His face was perfectly symmetrical and beautiful. His black hairline framed his slightly squared forehead. His pink lips wore well with his olive Puerto Rican skin. If he wasn't her father's best friend, Heather thought she could love him. Perhaps her emotions were particularly sensitive at the time, she guessed. Mrs. Whitney often left Heather alone with him, and she enjoyed it. He lay on his back and sometimes his brown eyebrow would give a little wrinkle, a little twitch. His brows looked like God stayed in the lines coloring him perfectly. His eyes looked like they wanted to open, but they wouldn't. A few times, he expressed a slight moan or gasp.

Just us, nobody around, Heather thought. She placed her hand on his. She felt a twitch, and in a startle, she took her hand off his. Things quieted down. She looked around. The air and surroundings were still. She placed her hand gently on his hand again, cupping her fingers around into his palm. She felt life in his hand. Twitching and something of warmth welcomed Heather to hold his hand. A couple of tears raced down her face, but she ignored them as she stared at Renato. Heather was sure that his mortal face was what made the Greek gods jealous. *He would be the one they would torment out of jealousy,* she thought. She stood beside him, bent down over him, and kissed his forehead. He didn't twitch, but Heather liked to think he looked happier. More peaceful. She was lighter and her heart skipped like it was jump-roping. The only man's forehead she ever kissed was Hugh's.

Heather then wondered if she could just as joyously kiss Renato's lips. No one was around, and he would never know. She peered out his bedroom window. Nobody was there.

Just Renato and me.

He kept his face and head completely still. Heather's heart pounded.

Oh, my goodness! She beamed as she thought of what she was about to do. She bent down, her face close to his, and she placed her lips on his soft lips and kissed him!

"What are you doing? Did you just kiss Renato?" Mae came into the room. "Is he awake?"

"No," Heather answered, "Where'd you"-

"You kissed a dying man?" Mae laughed and shot Heather a startled look. She kept staring at Heather and laughing, enjoying her embarrassment. Mae quieted down as she studied Renato's face. She walked over beside Renato, heightened to her tiptoes, leaned over Renato's face, and planted a kiss with a sucking sound on his lips.

"Mae! Stop!" Heather curtly shouted. Mae stood up, smiling at Heather.

"What? You did it!" She began to lean back over Renato. Heather pulled her back.

"Mae! Are you crazy? He's a grown man!" She stood up and stared at Heather as if shocked by her own actions. "Don't tell anyone, do you hear me? I will beat you!" Heather warned.

"Don't tell anyone what?" Mrs. Whitney came in the doorway with Veronica Nolan behind her. They both looked at Heather, waiting for an answer. Where did everybody come from?

"It's a secret, Mrs. Whitney. That means none of your business," Mae answered with wide eyes and the most stoic face Mae could pull off. Heather was relieved and as composed as she was able.

Mrs. Whitney, Mae, and Heather gravitated towards staying together, mostly at Renato's house.

"You know, Old Man Whitney - as you and everyone liked to call him — was fourteen years my senior," Mrs. Whitney told Heather. "We were in love every day."

Mrs. Whitney didn't mind if Heather or Mae smoked, and

she let Heather have shots of spirits anytime.

Mae and Heather cried themselves to sleep each night. Their pillows soggy, no Daddy, and Mrs. Whitney brought more news: "Your mother is on her way. She'll be here sometime tomorrow, I suspect." Mae smiled bigger than she had for some time. The sisters spent the rest of the day at home, cleaning and preparing for their Momma's arrival, another task to block out the hurt for Hugh. Heather hadn't brought herself to walk to the store. Not yet. Mrs. Whitney assured Heather that it stayed locked.

Heather dreamed; it'd be the three of them, Momma, Mae, and Heather. Three again, and besides the permanent ache in Heather's heart for Hugh, maybe not too different. Heather was sure as she cleaned that her Momma would stay. For good, like a Momma. Heather let her own dreams fall and sit quiet, but there was no loss of hope. Being with her mother felt like a wonderful dream. They'd eat together, and laugh together, and share stories like women shared. Their Momma would tell them stories, tell them more about her. Heather cleaned her parents' bedroom and the windows and wiped out every speck of dust she found. Cleaning the bedroom was bittersweet; Heather picked up Hugh's socks he pulled off when he got out of bed the last morning he was alive; but it was for Momma, so she'd feel at home.

Sylvia had left to live her own dream. Heather thought about that. Sylvia had to have known how Heather felt, as she now wanted to travel South for love and family. *Momma can guide me,* Heather planned. With her here, perhaps she would understand Heather's pull towards Savannah, and Mae would be happy to be left with her Momma. Each wipe and sweep got Heather closer to her dreams. Dreams added on to dreams.

10

Got Company

The following morning, Heather forgot her dream. She woke up in her own bed to a horrific tingling washing through her, and she smelled last night's remains of tears and runny nose on her pillow. Her room had been neglected since Hugh passed. The walls looked gray and didn't want to be seen. They didn't want her to leave, but to stay capped in depression with them. She sat up, enveloped in the dank and dim. She felt nauseated looking at the walls, and then she heard a tap ringing from the living room. *Like Daddy's coffee tin. . . Daddy!* She was still too sleepy to conjure reason. *It's Daddy! They were wrong. Everybody was wrong! He's fine. Just fine.* Excitement blew Heather out of the smelly room to the living room to see Hugh. She stumbled and tingled in a confused pain.

Her eyes smiled straight at Hugh's chair, where a Black woman sat. Their reunion wasn't the way Heather had dreamed it.

"Girl, about time! The sun done come up," she stared at Heather for a minute, and Heather stared back at her, both motionless. Sylvia continued to sit as the sun fumed a taunting yellow ray between the two women. Sylvia's legs were crossed, and she wore high heels, which looked uncomfortable in the low-sitting chair. Her knees protruded like her bodyguard. Heather was still slumbering, thinking her daddy was home and well. She didn't want to wake up to reality, to wicked reason.

Sylvia sighed and said, "Heather, stop looking at me like you don't know who I am. . . You look- . . . not so pretty." Mae created a scurry and a plop of feet in the bedroom. She pounced to the living room.

"Momma?" Mae's hair was smashed so much on one side, her head looked lopsided. She wore a small undershirt that exposed her belly and tight long underpants with her fat feet busting out of the bottoms. She didn't notice, or she didn't care. Her eyebrows were raised, looking for promise.

"Oh my—girl! Mae? . . . What'd Hugh do to you?" Sylvia scrunched her nose as if she just tasted something rotten. Heather stood beside Mae quietly in front of their mother, feeling vulnerable.

"Girls," Sylvia began with her eyes closed, and Heather stood still to hear whatever Sylvia wanted to tell her. Heather was nineteen. "Girls, what did Hugh do with the store key? The cops locked up the place, and I can't find the key."

"Daddy's dead," Heather answered in acceptance.

"Heather, I know he is dead! If he was still alive, don't you think I'd ask him myself?" She held out her hands to stop the girls from rousing a conversation.

"Look, girls," she kept going, "it's great to see you!" A smile exposed her beautiful teeth. Heather and Mae instinctively smiled back.

"Momma, are you taking us home to New York?" Mae asked with a mimicking smile. Mae called New York "home."

"Mae, we are home!" Heather snapped, realizing she and Mae had different dreams involving their Momma's arrival.

"Of course, Heather," Sylvia started. "Mae, your sister's right. I can't take you away from your home. That'd be unfair of me." She placed her hand over her chest like she was sharing her heart with her girls. She had a cigarette case sitting on the arm of Daddy's chair.

The girls promised to help Sylvia find the key, but Heather knew there was nothing to find.

Sylvia left for Renato's house across the street. Mae and Heather cleaned and got ready to go there, too. Mrs. Whitney rushed in quickly and told Heather and Mae to come that way soon. She was nursing Renato and trying to keep all the women away so he could rest.

"Alright, Mrs. Whitney. We'll be over soon," Heather assured her.

Heather sneaked to Sylvia's room and glanced through her suitcase. She had a flask that felt full. Heather opened it and sipped the whiskey inside. A golden scarf, some pantyhose, and her cigarette case. Heather secured the items in her room before leaving the house with Mae.

When they stepped on Renato's front yard, Mrs. Whitney motioned from the bedroom window for Mae and Heather to sneak in through the window. Mrs. Whitney's face was frozen in a horrific gaze of shock. Her eyes could have drooped more sadly down each side if they weren't rounded so widely in shock. Her lips looked like they were never made for smiling.

"Your mother is sitting in the living room, and Renato's awake!" she whispered. "Let's talk together without her in here."

Renato stirred awake; his eyes opened. Mrs. Whitney had already told him about Hugh. They heard Sylvia singing. Renato's eyes opened wider.

"Someone else is in my house. . . no, on the front porch, singing. . . My God, it's Sylvia!" Renato stated with a horrified expression.

"Heather, Mae, and I tended to you," Mrs. Whitney explained. She leaned forward with her hand patting on top of Renato's hand. His face was frozen, submitting to his sense of hearing Sylvia.

"Heather? . . . Mae?" Renato repeated and tried to sit up, but he winced and held his side. He then breathed loudly as if exhausted, and stated, "Hugh! Ah . . . no! Get her out of here!"

Mrs. Whitney told Heather he was disoriented but "he has to come out of it." She sat still as if something might break, or cry, if she moved. She was watching the events replay in his mind. But now, the present moment was so cruel, placing memories on Renato of Hugh — his best friend dying.

His breathing quickened into a gasp.

"Renato, lie back. Lie back, now. I know this is terrible. This is all terrible, . . . get it together. We've got to talk." Mrs. Whitney could turn from a soft teacake lady to a loaded gun, all meticulously planned. Heather felt like she was in the dark to something going on. She had been two years younger last time Sylvia was around, and Heather was imprisoned in a regression, knowing nothing, not knowing which way to go.

"Renato, now wake up . . . Renato . . ." Mrs. Whitney insisted. As soon as he tried to rise, Mrs. Whitney pulled his arm to help him sit up. Heather took his other arm. Mae gave him a cup of water. "How are you feeling? Good?" Mrs. Whitney asked.

"I hope so, Renato," Heather told him.

"I hope so, too," Mrs. Whitney said, "because you are needed and needed now!"

He slowly leaned up, then sat up with his feet over the bed.

"I'm sorry, Mrs. Whitney," Renato strained. "Who's she with?"

Mrs. Whitney looked down and answered, "She's alone."

In a few minutes, Renato recollected his body's perseverance to know how to stand. He stumbled across to the foot post and tried to regain his balance. He stood still. Heather took the liberty to light him a cigarette, and one for herself.

He took it and looked at her baffled, "Heather, thank you? Are you okay?" He lifted his arm slowly, as if trying to comfort her.

"I'm good, Ren," Heather lied. Her daddy was gone, and she sought clarity from her mother. Her chest and head filled with emotion and erupted into streams of tears.

"Renato, she wants to take care of you," Mrs. Whitney told him, wiping away a tear. "Ren, try to keep your temper."

"What about you, Mrs. Whitney?" Renato jested, returning to his old self.

Renato slowly slid his feet to the bedroom door. Mrs.

Whitney, Heather, and Mae followed him. He opened it and stared out toward the kitchen, where Sylvia sat with legs crossed, swinging a foot.

Sylvia stared at Renato placidly. He looked like he had already lost a fatal battle against her. She stood and shuffled her feet toward Renato with her arms out to embrace him.

"Oh, Renato!" she hugged and patted him, having to bend over a bit due to her height and her high heels. As she hugged him, Renato's eyes locked on Mrs. Whitney's. Mrs. Whitney shook her head with a stern *no*. Heather saw it.

Holding his shoulders, Sylvia stared at Renato with wrinkled eyebrows that confused Heather. She didn't see those wrinkled eyebrows of affection when they were at home. The realization staggered Heather's breath; she witnessed her mother mask apathy and shout vanity. *Does she like to wrinkle things?* Heather wondered and felt guilty for wondering so. Sylvia's mothering was unclear to Heather and rarely thought about. She did give birth to Heather, and Heather wanted to get out of Sterling herself. But this morning brought an uncomfortable perspective. She didn't like her mother.

"I'm so sorry," Sylvia whispered to Renato. A hate simmered within Heather, and she hated even that. She felt sick. She took a puff off the smoke and bolted outside to throw up. She quickly regained a sliver of strength and walked back into the quickened course of life, of all their lives.

"Renato, I'm needed back in the city – New York City, Renato. I can't stay. So," articulated lip movements compensated for Sylvia's lowered voice. Staring at Renato, she strolled a couple of steps toward the kitchen where Mrs.

Whitney stirred a pot of soup. "We need to quickly settle things regarding the store. You know, since it's now mine." She stood by an ignoring Mrs. Whitney. "Mrs. Whitney, how are you?"

Both of their husbands had been shot dead. The two widows were too different for this comparability to be perceived uncanny.

Sylvia wasn't staying, and she didn't see her daughters in the picture of the store's future. What a bolt of pain to feel unimportant. No family of three, just two — Mae and Heather. If numbness could hurt, Heather felt it. A building block of life was a hardened component of the heart, something Heather learned from her mother this day.

Renato slid his feet slowly through his kitchen. He tried to contain a grimace of pain from his face as he moved. He opened the ice box, which was empty. He let his body fall into a chair at the table. The soup simmered on the stove. Heather made two small bowls and gave one to Renato.

"You sure about that, Sylvia? I think it now belongs to the one and only Heather Randolph," Renato turned his eyes toward Mrs. Whitney and then Heather, "Mrs. Whitney, you think that's right?"

Heather was enthralled by the steadfastness Renato showed. Her eyes glanced over at her mother. She stared at Heather.

"Take what you want," Renato replied. "Hell, I don't care, Sylvia. I'm too weak to argue with you." He stopped as if he thought of something new. "When is Hugh's funeral?"

"It was two days ago," Mrs. Whitney said.

"Yes, so naturally I have to get back," Sylvia explained.

"Sylvia, your daughters"- Renato began.

"They are staying here," she quickly said. "They like it here. This is their home. I don't want to take them from the place they love." She smiled the same smile at Heather earlier that morning. Heather set her broth on the counter. It wasn't very hot, and the smell was strong. *I can make my own decisions, so please don't speak for me!* Heather wished she had spoken up.

"She hates this place, Sylvia," Renato said. "Mae, Heather," he raised his voice to grab attention, staring at Sylvia as he spoke to us, "have you spoken to your ma about where you wanna live?"

Momma quickly answered, "Of course we did. This morning. In their home. They remember, Renato. I'm not taking their home away from them. I'm not like that." She lifted the ladle full of broth up to smell.

"No. They know what you're like. I know what you're like," Renato's voice got louder, and he pounded his fist on the table. His face reddened and tightened. "Get the hell out of here!"

"Leave Momma alone, Renato!" sang out Mae's voice from the living room, and Sylvia turned around from the stove and smirked at Renato's startle.

"Oh," Renato replied, "well then. I'm sorry, Mae," he shouted from the kitchen. "Why don't you go back to the big city with your Momma?" Renato flinched and grabbed his side. He turned to Sylvia, "Why not, Sylvia?" Renato looked at Mrs. Whitney and Heather, pointing his finger at Sylvia. "She don't want em. She don't want her own kids."

"Shut up, Renato!" Mae stormed into the kitchen. "You don't know nothing!" Mae tightened her lips, glared at

Renato, and stomped back in the living room.

"Sylvia, leave," Renato said calmly. His breathing increased, and he slowly stood to his feet and scooted to the lavatory. Sylvia sat across the table from Mrs. Whitney.

"I'm sorry for your loss, Mrs. Whitney." Sylvia stared at Mrs. Whitney and added, "I mean, he never cared for me, now did he? But I'm sorry for you."

Mrs. Whitney glared at Sylvia and remained quiet. Sylvia began a song, *"I'd choose you again. Again, and again. . ."* That's my new signature piece. New York loves it. Pittsburgh does, too." She began singing again: *"We lose and we win, it's still us in the end. . ."* Old Man Whitney had nothing on New York City. You know that, Mrs. Whitney. That's the truth." Her eyes scrolled over to Heather and smiled at her.

Anger burst some energy in Heather, but she felt weaker. Mrs. Whitney sat still and fixated her eyes on Sylvia. Mrs. Whitney didn't reflect a nervous or scared twitch in her entire face.

"Mrs. Whitney, are you not speaking to me?" Sylvia poked.

"I promised Hugh never to use unkind words of their mother in their presence," Mrs. Whitney answered, staring back. "He said it wasn't fair to them."

"Oh, you care how she feels. You're her Momma now?"

Heather intervened, "I'm sitting right here, Momma, if there's something you wanna ask me."

With a slam of her hand on the table she sneered, "I see you! I see you!"

Heather slowly stood and walked into the living room to see Mae sitting on the couch staring at her. Mae sat in the dark with tired eyes, and her round, chubby face was longer. She looked at Heather with love and relief. No smiles. No expression at all, really, but Heather knew Mae was glad to see her. They both missed their Daddy, and the bickering tired them more. Mrs. Whitney joined them on the couch.

"The store—where's the key, Renato?" Sylvia snapped, hands on her hips. Renato returned, wincing and panting in pain. His eyes were glassy and his eyelids red.

"Hugh's dead, Sylvia," he stopped to catch his breath. "The father of your kids. . . He's dead. . . I told you to get out." Renato leaned back quietly. "Use Hugh's key," Renato answered. Hugh didn't have a key. Renato knew that. Hugh lost it so many times that he just let Renato lock and unlock the doors.

"Daddy didn't" —

"Shut up, Mae!" Heather whispered.

"Coroner probably has the items that were in his pocket. Try there, Sylvia," Mrs. Whitney spoke in a low voice. Sylvia left without a word.

Soon after, Heather walked home. She felt exhausted, and Mae and Mrs. Whitney tended to Renato.

Heather walked in the door, and Sylvia walked quickly to her from Hugh's room.

"Where's the damn key, girl? And what was that over there?" She pointed her long arm taut toward Renato's house. Heather had heard this tone from her just before Sylvia hit her. "Not a welcome, nothing! Sterling hasn't changed. My own flesh and blood acting so nasty!" She stood inches away from Heather's face, angry and still. Heather didn't have anywhere to go, nowhere to even step. Sylvia raised her cigarette case.

"I did find this under your nasty pillow!" Sylvia slapped Heather's face with both of her hands quickly, still holding the cigarette case. "Thief!" she shouted and popped Heather's ears and head as Heather crouched over.

Her hands angered into fists on Heather's back quickly like pellets, and she punched, descending Heather to the floor with both her hands. Heather quickly scrunched into a ball on the floor. Every spot she hit pulsed and burned and remembered her. Heather lay still with her face buried as she always had, feeling young and helpless again. She had a lot and nothing racing at the same time through her mind. She was insulted; she knew she didn't deserve her fists. Heather was a grown woman. Her father was dead, and her mother's hands had to stop. Heather's heart pumped frantically. She straightened up, growled, and punched Sylvia on the side of her head. Heather instantly regretted her unplanned action. It didn't relieve a bit of tension, and Heather felt lightheaded and nauseous. Heather was released, abandoned from having to love her mother, but she wanted to.

Amidst regaining awareness, Heather didn't know where Sylvia was. Finally, in gasps of breath, Sylvia managed out, "An embarrassment, you are!"

Sylvia's voice was at the kitchen table, a distance away. Heather stood still with her feet a bit wider apart, like she was trying to keep standing. She inhaled a gasp, slightly for a small second — she could feel it -- when she looked at her mother.

"Stop it, Momma," Heather shook out, and her eyes filled with tears.

Sylvia confirmed there was no need for Heather to be

imprisoned with such hope. Heather didn't have to hold on anymore. She could have, and probably should have, felt free. Alone, bruised, unwanted, sad, and free. But Heather didn't feel free at all. Sylvia was her mother, and Heather loved her.

Mae came busting in the door with a loud "Hey, Momma!" She stood by Heather staring at Sylvia, grinning like all her dreams came true. "Hey, Momma!" she repeated, like maybe her poor Momma didn't hear Mae the first time. Heather slipped out of the kitchen toward her room. She walked to her room feeling awkward as if she shouldn't have stood upright to get there. She wondered if moving along on her hands and knees would have been more comfortable.

Heather needed her dream. To go to Savannah where no one knew she was once a little girl. They'd meet her as a woman, and there, she'd act like a woman. She'd find her black singing man. She imagined the air to have a romantic green tint.

"What do you want, Mae?" Momma snapped, sitting at the kitchen table.

"Nothing. I ate some of Mrs. Whitney's soup. Did you?"

"No."

"Why not?"

No answer.

"I'll go get you some if you want me to. I'll punch Ren's face, too."

"Yeah, go get me some."

Mae came back a few minutes later. Heather was lying in bed fully awake.

"Hey, Momma!" The inflection in her voice tried extra hard to show Sylvia how loved she was. Heather didn't hear any footsteps; Mae must have been standing still.

"Momma?' Mae tried, "There's some man who asked where Sylvia was. I told him 'That's my Momma!' and he's coming up the yard now."

11

The Marsh Rabbit

"Stay in your room, and let me visit with my friend," Sylvia told Mae.

"Who's that?" Mae asked.

"Mind your own business! It's my friend. Go on to your room."

Mae stood waiting for an answer from her mother.

"He's my manager for my singing career, so go on!"

Heather and Mae looked out the window from their bedroom at a man with a swollen belly wearing a bow tie and suspenders, rocking from left to right with each step. Sylvia and the man stood in the yard exchanging no cordial greeting, no smiles, and they walked together up the porch and inside the house.

"About time," Sylvia said, "The kids . . . and everything." The man's voice mumbled something; the girls couldn't make it out. Sylvia said, "I can't find the key to the store. . ." More mumbling. "I'm headed to the magistrate now. Take me there." Sylvia was a stranger to Heather. She and the other stranger stood in her personal life, and they walked out the door without a goodbye, which strangers are allowed to do.

"Mae!" Heather hollered, "Who was that?"

"I don't know," she shrugged her shoulders and stared at Heather like she might tell Mae who he was.

"Well, what'd he say?"

"He just wanted to know where Sylvia was and I said, 'My Momma?'" Mae smiled as she spoke, "and that was it." Her whole face kept smiling.

"I'm tired. You wanna nap with me?" Heather slept more after Hugh's death. Tears acted like a sleep potion.

Before lying down, Heather walked into Hugh's bedroom and found Sylvia's suitcase. She found a book of matches. She tucked it into her own suitcase under her bed, lay down again, and fell asleep.

She awoke hearing Sylvia and the strange man on the front porch. Mae wasn't in the bedroom.

"I don't want things this way! No!" Sylvia sounded frustrated.

"Shut your mouth!" gruffed the man's voice. It was airy with annoying enunciation in each word. Heather leaned her head closer to the window to hear the conversation. The man continued, "Don't let 'em hear us! Just listen one second, listen to me — they . . . are . . . your . . . ticket, Sylvie! Your special ride to fame! Come on, honey! Get with it! Many celebrities play that sympathy card to get noticed. And they do! They sure do!"

"I don't want to haul them around," Sylvia responded.

"Sylvie, you not thinkin'! Sylvie, they old enough to fend

for themselves. We'd just make them come around for publicity. For the camera, for the newspapers and magazines! And to keep their mouths shut. Beat 'em good a few times, and they'll listen. Especially the oldest."

Heather gasped and froze still until she fell back asleep.

The next morning, Heather awoke to a knock on her bedroom door. Sylvia and the strange man stood at the doorway.

"You ain't got no right looking in my bedroom!" Heather shouted with a morning scratch in her voice. She was sure Hugh would have told him the same thing.

Sylvia soothed in with soft steps and told her friend, "She's just trying to wake up. Don't mind her. . . Heather? . . . Heather? Wake up. I've got some special news, girls." Heather sat up in bed. Mae appeared and skipped in between Sylvia and the man; she faced them to hear the news, standing close to Sylvia. The man stared another second under the brim of his fedora. He held on to his suspenders under his over-sized wool coat as if he held on to a gun holster for a draw. Mae placed her arms on her mother's waist. Sylvia pulled Mae's arms down slowly and said, "Now listen. How about I take my girls home with me to live in New York City!" Mae stood in frozen excitement for a second and shouted in glee. She forced her arms around Sylvia and pulled Sylvia's body to her cheek. A bruise on Heather's arm she collected earlier felt like it had a painful pulse in it. She felt other spots, too, like on her cheekbone and on her other arm.

As Sylvia pulled Mae away from her, she stared at Heather and said, "Sulky girl!" She lengthened the moment of her disapproving glare. "You can start packing. We leave tomorrow morning." Her face was a stone as she stared at Heather. She turned around and strutted away.

"I'm nineteen. I'm not going!" Heather tried to holler louder than she actually did.

"You're not staying with me?" Mae asked, trapping Heather. Heather wanted to answer that she wouldn't need to stay with Mae; she'd be with her momma, but Heather couldn't leave her sister with a stranger. Momma's friend widened his eyes at Mae's statement, like he enjoyed the entertainment. He shook his head with a smirk and followed Sylvia out of the room. Mae was so excited she couldn't stop talking.

"Can you close your stupid mouth?" Heather said. Mae grabbed clothes and her brush and her soap and threw stuff on the bed. Other than a glare at Heather, she didn't answer. Heather sat still on the bed; Mae swished through the room in bliss.

"Should I pack my rollers or get some more in New York?" she asked Heather.

"I don't know, and I don't care."

Heather didn't pack. She sat. She wondered how Renato was doing. She hadn't been to see him since yesterday morning. Mae half-sung and half-hummed a song as she scanned the room for good things to pack.

She tried to cheer Heather up.

"She's our mother. We have to love her." Mae may have been right, and Heather realized it. But thoughts of her mother's probable plans clouded hope. Sylvia would sell the store to the town of Sterling, stuff her pockets, and reach for the stars.

A new plan perked Heather to sit up in her bed. She needed to find Renato. She didn't know where her shoes were, and she didn't feel up to looking for them. She heard her mother squeak a laugh in the kitchen. Heather felt like there was a dark shadow laughing and pressing her back down to accomplish nothing, to care about whatever others cared about. Her upright back turned into a slump. Heather stared at nothing in front of her, motionless. She decided she was tired and fell back asleep.

"What are you doing on Hugh's front porch!" Heather heard Renato's angry voice approaching the front yard. "Get off!" She heard a rumbling and peered out her bedroom window. She saw a wooden chair land on its side in the front yard. She heard her mother snap at Renato in protest. Her mother's friend picked the chair upright and sat in the chair in the yard. "I'm here to see the girls. Are they home?" A stoic voice towards Sylvia, and Heather didn't hear her mother answer for a few seconds - no doubt she was staring at Renato enjoying that he wanted something from her, even if it was a simple answer of her children's whereabouts. Sylvia was running the time.

Mae asked Heather to roll her hair. She sat on the floor in front of Heather. Heather stared at the top of Mae's head and diligently folded over the shiny hair onto a roller, tight and secure.

They heard their mother's voice muffled through the window, "Yes, Renato. Please, go see them. And you should make every minute count. I just can't bear to part from my girls," Sylvia sounded like she was reading a movie script, "so they're going back to the city with me, their poor widow

Momma."

"Sylvia, did you hear? Hugh's killer's been found," Renato said.

"Is that so?" Sylvia commented.

"Dead. That's what I was told."

"Really, Ren? Who's your source, a corn-cropper?"

"Said the same man killed Old Man Whitney."

The front door opened and closed. Renato came to the bedroom door and stopped. The absence of Hugh was still a fresh grief for him. He looked around the room unsettled. But for Mae and Heather, seeing Renato reminded them of their Daddy and of when life was normal and good. Renato looked tired. Heather stood up and hugged him gently, mindful of the bandages.

"Only good-hearted men should wear bow ties, so I never wore one," he said. "I don't like that guy."

"Hey, Ren. Come on in," Mae and Heather welcomed him. He sat on the other corner of their bed. His eyebrows were serious, holding a bothersome notion in his thoughts. Mae and Heather tried to act casual and as normal as they could remember how. They had both kissed him, and he had no idea. Heather was thinking about it and wondered if Mae was, too.

"Ren, after I finish Mae's hair, I need to speak with you in private," Heather said.

"Can't I listen?" Mae asked.

"No," Heather answered. She looked at Renato; he was staring down at space, his deep thoughts somewhere down there.

"I remember as a boy," Renato began, "I stood on a knoll,

you know. It was down at the marsh."

"In Georgia?" Mae asked.

"Yeah, in Georgia. Anyway," Renato stared ahead like he could see it. "I watched this little mother marsh-rabbit trailing to find her baby, but it was in the deep marsh, you know. In the tall grasses."

"A what?" Mae interrupted.

"A marsh rabbit, Mae. These fast little rabbits back home. Shut up and listen. . . Anyway, she found her baby, and she got it to follow her out of the marsh, you know, where it wasn't in danger anymore." At these words his face color darkened. "They camouflaged with the mud floor, and so I had to concentrate, really concentrate, to track them. But still, that tall marsh could have swallowed them whole. Foxes, coyotes, crocodiles, hawks — they all wait on fools like these two."

"They get eaten?" Mae asked.

"Shut up, Mae!" Heather told her. "What's the point here?" Heather wondered, *Is Momma the marsh-rabbit? Are you, Ren? I'm not the baby rabbit, am I?*

Renato continued, "Well, they ran, Heather. Blind leading the blind. She and her baby, full speed at the mercy of whatever predators lay in their path. No time to think about it. They just had to go." Renato looked over at Mae and Heather. He placed his hands together in his lap, fidgeting his fingers and tapping his heels.

"I watched, thinking surely something would snap — sharp teeth or a claw — you know, at the little rabbits before they got out of there. They ran in the thick marsh. I don't know what happened to them." He picked up a roller pin and observed it in his fingers. "Is it courage or stupid when you go forward blindly?" He then looked at the girls again. Heather thought he seriously wanted an answer.

"What the hell are you talking about, Ren?" Mae asked. "You're stupid wherever you go. You ain't talking about Momma, are you?"

"Not even thinking of her, Mae," Renato told her. "She's always stupid."

"Are you on something, Ren?" Mae asked, "Mrs. Whitney keeping you medicated?"

Renato smiled and answered, "Yeah, I'm numb. Do I really sound stupid?"

"Yes, Ren. You sound real stupid," Mae answered, ultimately at the chance to call Renato stupid.

"Heather, . . . Mae," Renato dragged out his words, "The man that shot Hugh was found. He's dead. He was found dead in Pittsburgh a couple of nights ago. I'm glad he's dead."

Heather and Mae were glad, too, they supposed, but the traces of grief still dwelt within. Is there any such thing as closure on the intangible? Hugh once said forgiveness was the only closure in life. "But I haven't got that one figured out just yet," Hugh once told Heather, "Too many hurtful layers to handle. Even for a handsome Negro man like me." Heather didn't have it figured out either. She didn't forgive her Daddy's killer; she wished she could've been the one to shoot him. She missed her father. He'd know what to say on sensitive topics that made Heather cry. She needed to get out of Sterling.

"Renato, can we speak?" Heather asked and motioned towards the back door. She followed Renato and combed her fingers down her wild hair and straightened the collar of her dress. He continued to the backyard, holding his side. The back door shut closed. They stood in the dull, cold air under a white sky, facing each other. Illinois was settling into freezing temperatures, and the day was still and quiet. Despite the murder of Hugh and the heavy family disruption, standing in the empty back yard alone with Renato staring at her arose an ecstatic emotion within Heather for a flash. Three wooden square crates of dirt waited on the ground by the door. Hugh placed seeds of some kind in the crates back in the spring. A couple of tan shriveled stems were collapsed in the dry dirt. They had tried.

"I'm sorry, Heather," Renato started.

"Renato, I'm not going to New York with Momma, and I need for you to help me."

"Heather, . . . what? What do you mean?"

"Are you still going to Savannah?"

"Yeah, I have to. I don't trust your mother."

"Take us, Ren! Me and Mae, away from here! You told Daddy you were going to Savannah, right? Daddy knew I wanted to go, too. So, take us!" Heather tried to keep her voice low, the stillness outside was so quiet and inconsiderate. She looked down at the crates of noiseless dirt. "We could even tell Mae we're going to New York. She wouldn't have to know. Not yet anyway."

"Heather, yeah, but . . . no."

"I can't be the marsh rabbit, Ren! I want to take Mae, but I can't do it alone. I need your help."

"Heather, I kinda thought I was the brave marsh rabbit. But then I thought of the sharp teeth, and" —

"Momma will figure it out once we don't come home," Heather whispered again, "and she'll be relieved, free to live her life. Don't you think? I just gotta lie to Mae to get her out the door. Is that wrong?"

"Heather! That's not it! You don't understand," Renato looked disappointed.

"Well, what was that whole story about the marsh rabbit?"

"I don't know, okay! I thought it through — stupid idea!" Renato replied. "Heather, it's dangerous to travel with me."

"Nice out," Heather didn't lower her voice anymore. "An apology for being you. A ticket for you to just walk away!" Heather popped the door open with a bang and stomped to her bedroom.

Mae blared, "Heather, you're going! Yes, you are! You can't leave me by myself, and you said you'd try and love Momma. So shut up, Heather!"

"No, . . . I didn't! Mae, . . ." Heather was stuck. She couldn't move her feet to go anywhere. Hugh needed her to not be like her Momma and not leave him, to help him care for Mae and the house and the store. She couldn't move except to go around and around. She knew she was a loyal daughter, and now a loyal sister. And now resentful. *Like my Momma, probably.*

12

Blackmail

The afternoon looked like the morning. Mae was busy packing, and Heather left for the store without telling Mae. The walk was easy. She didn't see nor meet eyes with a soul. She walked in every dark spot and shadow in front of her along the way in hopes of hiding.

When the store came into her sight, it broke her heart. It stood alone and waited for its family to come laugh and love inside while it held everyone. So forlorn and abandoned. The front table still held baskets, and Hugh's chair was empty. He wasn't hiding behind his black skin. Heather and the store connected like two best friends. Childhood memories were in that building; they weren't gone. Heather appreciated the hope to start her grown-up life that came alive in the store. Her skin was damp with a chill as she came closer. *Stay focused, Heather!* The horrors of the murder scared her as she placed her hand on the front doorknob, and then around to the back. Both locked.

She found an unlocked window that usually stayed unlocked. She slipped in, knocking down a display of boxes of something, erupting a ruckus that stung her nerves. The store felt like an ice box. Inside was dark despite the outside brightness. She waited until her eyes could make out the silhouettes of shelves and counter corners before she moved. The store smelled like an over-ripe onion; the vegetables had aged, the ones they'd give away, throw out, or eat permeated their odors. She paused, and she didn't turn on any lights. Her heart pounded in her chest. She could see the silhouette of the murderer in her memory, standing at the counter with a gun.

"Daddy?" she called out to the void. She sunk her head down to the edge of the counter and wept for a moment, releasing the resurfaced pain.

In the dark, the back office was difficult to find. She kept turning around, not convinced that the silhouette of the murderer wasn't real. She panted. Moving slowly, she still knocked over glass jars and cans. Paired with this bedlam should have been her Daddy's voice: *Heather! What this time?* She needed the comfort of his voice. In the back office, she found Hugh's matches and lit a candle for light. She slowly pulled out the long bottom drawer of a filing cabinet. In the back of the drawer was a box labeled "Cleaning Rags." Heather opened the box. She grabbed all the cash inside and placed the money in a burlap bag Hugh had left on the cabinet.

She believed she had to take the money. Her mother couldn't find the keys, so Heather was sure Sylvia planned to do what Heather was doing. Sylvia came for nothing but money; Heather couldn't believe otherwise. Whatever emotions Heather felt had to be set aside for the task at hand. She knew where Hugh hid all his cash. The take was easy, but still unsettling. But it was the only help she had.

Just as Heather set motion to leave, glass from a side window shattered. Heather stooped down and blew out the candle. Someone was breaking in. *The silhouette? Momma? Her bow-tie friend? The murderer?* Heather didn't know what to do, and she started panting as quietly as she could. She could run out the back door, but she couldn't move; fear froze her. A noise from her may result in getting shot. So she stayed as still and as quiet as she could. Footsteps moved closer to the back office. Closer to Heather. *Maybe a partner in Daddy's murder. Maybe the killer wasn't dead! Who was it?* Items within the store crashed with more violence than Heather had accidentally managed. A forcible, intentional destruction with wails and growls. Whoever was in the store knew the store was closed and knew the owner was dead. The footsteps knew where the office was. At the office door, the footsteps stopped and Heather's heartbeat faster. She could hear her breath, and she wondered if the robber could as well. A match was swiped across its book, and there was light. Heather looked to see a match in the hand of Renato. Heather saw him before he saw her. Her presence on the floor startled him, and he grabbed the door frame in shock. He bent down beside Heather. His sleeves were rolled up.

"Heather!" he laughed quietly. "What are you doing here?"

Renato was there for the money. Renato swore it was for Heather. Although incredulous, they both wanted to keep Sylvia from having it. But Heather's guard elevated against Renato. Renato had blood on his hand from breaking a window.

Heather asked, "Why'd you have to tear the place up because I heard you intentionally making a mess, huh?

Why?" He didn't answer; Heather continued, "The broken stuff is now less of what I own. You need to know that."

Renato stood and stared before he answered. "Yeah, I'm sorry." Renato blew out the match as they stood. "I wasn't thinking."

"My Daddy, a Negro man, worked hard to keep this store opened, but you know what, Ren? I'm too tired to argue with you." Heather leaned against the counter and lifted her burlap bag.

"Where's the deed, Heather? She'll be after that, too," Renato reached to a hook where his store keys hung from the last day he worked. "This is why I broke a window," he said, dangling his keys. They agreed to search for it together, but they couldn't find a deed.

"I remember Daddy saying the deed was hidden. In Savannah with Mr. Haverson, maybe?" They didn't find it at the store.

"We've done our damage," Renato said.

"I don't think so, Renato," Heather had an impulsive epiphany. She felt these seconds sitting on the edge of a possible next chapter in her life. "You come into *my* store — *my* store, Renato! And you planned to take *my* money and then run off to Savannah without taking the one woman who wants to go more than anybody, and with her money? Then fine! You go on to Savannah! Try anyway! I'll just report you for stealing from *my* store. Since you don't want to take me with you."

"What the hell are you saying, Heather? I said I was sorry, didn't I?" Renato paced in the little office. Turning his head side to side as if someone else was breaking in.

"You hear me. You have a choice. Take Mae and me to Savannah with you. Now, and you're free. Or leave us, and I will tell the police you stole from Dodge Grocers."

"No! No, you won't, Heather! I'm not taking you nowhere! No, forget it," Renato walked out of the office and grabbed a pack of cigarettes. "So, you'll put me in jail if I don't take you to Savannah with me?"

"That's right. You be my marsh mother rabbit, or I'll be the predator, yes." Heather laughed at her own wit. She was threatening a family friend, and she was reeking of enmity. It didn't feel good, risking a long-time relationship. However, he wrecked the store, and that encouraged her and reminded her how she wanted what she wanted. What did he want that was any different from Sylvia? Renato was in the crossfire. She almost couldn't stand herself.

"You've never been out of Illinois, and you want to go to Georgia? You don't know what you're asking, Heather."

Heather knew he was the one who didn't know what she was asking. Heather wanted to go where no one knew she was a little girl once. Where no one saw her as helpless and dependent, embarrassing herself. And even if she sometimes acted that way, she didn't want to be seen as anyone other than a woman.

"Well, I'm leaving this evening," Renato said. "Mrs. Whitney's dropping me off at a bus station. Old Man Whitney, he meant well, but I gotta get out of here, back home. Tonight." Renato stood and watched as Heather filled her bag with store goods.

"You in trouble, Ren?"

"I don't know," Renato said and rubbed the back of his

neck. "Don't worry about it."

They unlocked the back door, walked out, and Renato locked the door behind them. Ironic.

"I guess I'll pick you two up at five. We'll start with a nice dinner," Renato said and smiled softly, politely. Heather supposed he had no choice. They split their route to their separate homes, and Heather walked away, away from the store. She carried the burlap bag of money, cigarettes, matches, apples, and snack cakes, anything to relieve her feeling of discontent. She didn't turn around to see the store. She didn't want it to speak to her.

When she got home, Sylvia was gone. Mae said she "looked mad," and she'd swing by and pick them up the next morning and to be ready. That they were old enough to fend for themselves for dinner, she told Mae. As if Heather didn't already feed them daily and had been for most of her life. Heather told Mae they were eating with Renato. She wondered where her Momma was going. Perhaps the store.

Mae and Heather dolled up for their dinner date. Mae did so blindly. She danced and sang and kept busy.

"*Hi-de hi-de hi-de-hi, Hey-de hey-de hey-de hey . . .*" she belted. Heather stuffed her suitcase with items Sylvia left laying around, her lipstick, another scarf. She must have taken her cigarette case with her. They placed their packed suitcases at the front door as Renato suggested.

Funny how Heather thought Mae was the one in the dark. Heather was running through the marsh, too.

13

Different Directions

*A*t five o'clock, Mrs. Whitney rolled her car in front of the Randolph house. The girls slid on their shoes and set their suitcases on the front porch — "like Momma asked us to" — that's what Heather told Mae. Renato ambled over, opened the back car door, and stood by it, waiting on the girls. Heather walked out the front door ahead of Mae and took the first steps of her life. Her feet felt light descending down the porch stairs with her skirt dancing with glee around her legs. Her big painted eyes viewed everything in front of her. A smile came naturally on her face to Renato, but Renato didn't smile at back at her.

He took off his hat — Hugh's hat. Heather remembered it sat on the counter in the store office. His hair was slicked back and shiny, and he should have smiled. Heather noticed a bright red line across the back of his hand, a fresh cut.

"Where's Mae?" Renato asked.

"Taking her sweet time." Heather answered and got into

the backseat.

"Mae!"

Mae slowly pranced out, every step with a purpose to own the moment. She sang out, "You looking sweet as berries, Ren. What happened to your hand?"

"Are you ready?" Renato leaned on the opened back car door, and Mae slid in beside Heather.

"I've got more to pack. I'll do it later," she responded. "Ren, you're ignoring my question. What happened to your hand?" she responded. He shut the door, but he didn't get in the front right away.

Mrs. Whitney complimented on how nice the girls looked, their hair, their dresses. They quit paying attention to Renato. Heather fixed her eyes on her home. She had helped her dad install the new metal doorknob on the front door just three years ago. It took the place of a wooden one, and Heather and Hugh agreed it gave the whole house a better look. She looked at her bedroom window. She could see the wall beside the bedroom door that never wanted her to leave. She hadn't made her bed before they left. She stared at the window and tried to rest her eyes on its contents, the same window where she often dozed off to sleep and dreamed of being on the other side of it.

Finally, Renato was in the car, still not smiling, like he was going to work.

Mrs. Whitney drove off.

They pulled away from the only home Heather and Mae ever knew. Heather looked back. The wide empty road where their three homes sat extended like an arm to hold her. If it whispered "stay," she'd hear it. The abandoned homes sat lonely, like Dodge Grocers. A heavy feeling filled her chest. She was taking the time to love her home, even to grieve the loss in a way, but Mae was ignorant of it all. She didn't know she'd not be back. Mae looked ahead, out her window, or at one of her fellow passengers, with no need to appreciate any of it.

Mae didn't ask again about his hand. "Where are we going to eat?" asked Mae.

"I need a drink, and then I need your help," Renato said to Mrs. Whitney, ignoring Mae again. Mrs. Whitney looked at him unconcerned.

"This is the safest way, Renato," Mrs. Whitney said. "You've got a good heart, Renato, so stop looking so mean."

"He obviously doesn't have a heart. He's not married and he's got no kids," Mae directed from the back seat. "And he won't answer a single damn question." Renato gave her a stoic look behind a contained laugh.

"What are you gonna do?" Renato asked Mrs. Whitney.

"I'm not the target," Mrs. Whitney answered. "You are."

The target to what? thought Heather. She blackmailed Renato, but she wasn't aiming to hurt him.

Renato pulled a folded paper from his pocket, then a pen from inside his coat. He unfolded the paper. "I need to write Ma. You think a letter can get to her quick enough?" Renato asked Mrs. Whitney.

"Quick enough for what?" she asked. Heather wondered the same thing.

"Quick enough. You know. Before any news gets down to her."

"Sure, it will," Mrs. Whitney was serious and positive in all her responses tonight. Renato rolled up his sleeves, bowed over his paper, and wrote. Silence and the consistent hum of the motor filled the car.

"They need you, Renato," Mrs. Whitney continued a few minutes later. "You're needed, and if that's a burden, accept it. They turn into something. Something worthy. Burdens usually do." Burdens?

"Who needs you, Ren?" Heather asked. She was offended by being considered a burden. Her thoughts took off in too many directions. *I don't need Renato. . . I left Momma, so I'll leave him. . . I can find my way to Savannah without him, and I'll tell him.* Her emotions flared.

"Ren, you making plans I don't know about?" Heather asked.

"No," he answered. "Are you?"

"Ren, it sounds like you're planning . . . something. Just tell me."

He turned his head sideways, "Well, I'm not." He turned around and stared at Heather with a puzzled look on his face. She was reassured, but she shifted her eyes from Mrs. Whitney to Renato.

"If you're not going to dinner with us, we'll just go with Mrs. Whitney. We got all dressed up and everything!" Mae added.

"I'm sorry, Heather and Mae," Mrs. Whitney said loudly over the motor, staring straight ahead at the road.

Renato told her, "Mrs. Whitney, it's fine." He looked back at the girls. "I'm hungry. Let's eat."

Burdens and targets, who was who?

14

Stationed

Mrs. Whitney parked in an empty spot right by the street. The place wasn't busy, but there were enough cars driving by, parking, and leaving, filled with destinations and beginnings and ends, to assure the road it still had a purpose. They were just west of Chicago.

Mrs. Whitney wasn't going into the restaurant with Renato, Heather, and Mae. Everyone got out of the car, and Mrs. Whitney gave each of them a long hug. Renato rolled down his sleeves and put on his sports coat and a dark brown wool trench coat over his whole attire.

"Heather, keep your smarts about you. Watch after Renato," Mrs. Whitney spoke softly to Heather as Renato held Mae's attention. Heather chose not to think about whether or not she would see Mrs. Whitney again. There was no time for speaking reason with Mrs. Whitney. What she should do, what she should think. Heather didn't even know where she was at. She could have turned any direction to go south and end up in China. She had to trust Renato.

Renato explained to Mrs. Whitney that his brother Isaac would "hopefully" pick them up a couple of bus stations away.

"I still haven't spoken to him, not yet, but I sent word from your phone, Mrs. Whitney," Renato said, adjusting his fedora.

The last expression on a face is how one is remembered; Mrs. Whitney had to have known her wistful, worried look unsettled the departure. Heather noticed her wrinkled eyebrows and resting frown. Mrs. Whitney's face was still tense when she smiled goodbye. Mrs. Whitney was a truthful woman, but she was hiding something, Heather was certain.

The restaurant rested on a corner of a lit-up town lined with two and three-story buildings and a long line of streetlights down sidewalks. Heather and Mae had been to a few restaurants before, but the newness kept them wide eyed and smiling. The owner of the restaurant ran a posh diner on the first floor, and a speakeasy bar in the basement. This owner allowed Mae and Heather to sit at the table despite their color. He was friends with Mrs. Whitney and Renato. Dinner kept all three of them in good spirits, and Heather forgot about life.

"I'm gonna try and call Isaac again," Renato left Heather and Mae at the table. Heather tried not to look around at other tables, because each time she did, someone stared at her. Maybe they didn't. She was new, and all these people were new. She wished Renato would hurry.

"What's wrong with you?" Mae didn't hide her stare towards Heather.

"Nothing. Nothing's wrong." Heather answered. Renato finally waltzed back in.

"Hey, girls," Renato chimed coolly. "We'll take the bus tonight." A handsome humility rested on his face, but his neck sloped forward and his head bowed. The girls didn't know any questions to ask — just follow Renato.

After dinner, Renato spoke with the restaurant owner for a few minutes, and they were led to the back of the restaurant. Their suitcases were sitting against a hallway wall along with a cloth bag of Renato's. Plans were made ahead; part of those plans were for Heather to follow. She had no choice.

The confirmation of following Renato rang in rounds in her mind.

Renato quickly said, "We need to hold on to these."

"What? I thought we had to leave them on the front porch," Mae said, and dread of lying to Mae edged upon Heather.

"Are we headed to New York City right now?" Mae acted like she discovered a prize, "Is Momma coming with us?"

Renato looked around and didn't answer, but he motioned for the girls to follow him. Follow him where? He wasn't supposed to be Heather's boss; they were traveling together. She demanded his eyes as she adamantly motioned a head shake, but he ignored her. They continued swiftly down the sidewalk.

"Renato?" Heather called. A frosty breeze relentlessly pushed their faces. Renato kept walking a foot in front of Heather, and Heather and Mae held their suitcases and followed him. He carried his bag on his back.

"Renato!" Heather repeated. She put a little hesitation in each step until she finally stopped. They were following a man known to have connections with the mob. Furthermore, he reassured his mother in a letter that he hadn't killed anybody — *what's he capable of?* Heather wondered. He did illegal stuff and knew illegal people. Mae saw Heather's worry.

"Ren," Heather pleaded; and not knowing what else to say, she repeated, "Ren." Renato stopped at a corner street of an intersection. Cars blared headlights frequently, and other walkers scattered purposely, invariably. Heather, Mae, and Renato were incognito and, in the midst, where all the shadows looked like a mess of black paint, outlining suspicion. Renato turned around and finally faced Heather. She asked, "Ren, where we going?"

"The bus station, Heather. You okay?" he asked.

"Ren," Heather started, "I'm not good." She felt something resembling a scream or a panic or a loud cry surfacing from her stomach and heart to her face. Renato peeled her suitcase out of her hand and set it on the sidewalk pavement.

"She don't wanna go to New York, Ren," Mae answered with raised eyebrows.

Renato cupped his hands on Heather's shoulders and stared at her. A few people crossed the streets toward them and walked past. A dome of streetlight hovered over them. Cars passed them sparingly, Renato looked around with wide eyes. "Heather, you just have to trust me please. I need to move fast, right? Please, trust me. But don't worry. And follow me and keep up. Do you want me to hold your case?" He picked up her suitcase.

"Carry mine, too," Mae said. Renato picked up her case in his other hand. They crossed a street, and they continued down the sidewalk toward the darkness, like another galaxy Heather wasn't aware of.

Mae skipped as if each step was closer to New York City. Were they? Trust him? Like a false prophet, straight to hell, or New York. Same thing as far as Heather was concerned.

"Heather, shut up and trust me," Renato stated, looking straight ahead as he walked.

Mae smiled wide. "She didn't say anything, Ren!"

"I can hear her thoughts," Renato answered.

The bus station building was long with tired pink bricks. Two buses huffed impatiently with rattling motors in front of the station.

"Three tickets to Savannah, Georgia," Renato stated lowly and leaned in closer to the ticket window in hopes Mae wouldn't hear. She paid him little attention. He gave the ticket man the two suitcases. Heather observed the bus attendant strip tags on the suitcases and write "To Savannah" on the strips.

With tickets in hand, Renato led Heather and Mae to board the bus. Heather and Mae found their seats. Renato sat two rows back. Heather looked back at Renato. He stared at Heather and Mae like he knew something horrible. He scratched his jaw, and Heather noticed his forehead shining with sweat. He scoped the outdoors, either hoping for something or dreading something. Passengers ambled their way on the bus slowly, taunting Heather's slimming patience for the next thing to happen. She wondered why she trusted anybody so passively, grossly. Maybe it was all she knew. She didn't want to be a grown woman who followed and didn't ask any questions.

Finally, everyone was seated, suitcases were stored underneath the bus floor, and the aisle was clear and settled.

The bus driver stood and walked down the aisle, stopping beside Renato. His back was to Heather and Mae, so Heather couldn't hear him, but he turned around and glanced cordially, not at Heather and Mae but over the tops of their heads. He turned around to speak lowly to Renato another minute. Renato then stood up and motioned with a tilt of his head that they were getting off the bus. Heather and Mae stood up in unison at the silent command. Heather knew why; their color disqualified them; that's just how it went. They walked back up the aisle to the front of the bus between passengers sitting comfortably and ready.

Others must have known more than Heather and Mae knew. Heather didn't know what though. There had to have been something of the world that was figured out, conclusions made. Everyone she walked between knew. Heather was not only incapable of knowing this truth, but she was in the way of these passengers, on their own journeys, trying to reach their own destinations. Heather was in the way. Something, . . . there was something —or maybe someone— in charge of telling everybody what the truth was. So, everyone knew something, and Heather knew they were wrong, but she didn't know who to stand up to, nor how to. She walked in between the all-knowers.

"Did we get on the wrong bus?" Mae asked. Heather glared back at her; Mae knew they didn't. Renato didn't answer. He placed Hugh's hat on his head, strolling like he was gracing the bus floor with his steps. He skipped down the steps of the bus. Heather and Mae followed him straight to the ticket window.

"Yes, the Negro bus will leave at 5:00 am," said the ticket

man. Renato let out an irritated chuckle and looked down defeated.

"And I'm allowed on the colored bus, yes?" Renato asked.

"It'll be fine," answered the ticket man.

"I won't get kicked off? I'm not colored," Renato returned.

"No sir, you'll be fine."

"Well, that's confusing. You sure?" Renato's voice mellowed to his angry tone, like when Hugh used to lecture Renato about fighting. "You realize this makes no sense, don't you?"

"If Mrs. Whitney was with us, she'd take us home," Mae said.

The bus of the all-knowers rolled away, along with the second bus, along with their luggage. Heather had her pocketbook of money, snacks, and cigarettes that she refused to put down. Renato still had his backpack. Heather, Mae, and Renato sat on a bench under a streetlight in front of the station like props assuring life at the empty station. A firehouse stood quietly across the street staring at them. Behind the bus station was grayness, possibly a flat field of nothing but speckled black air. Mae sat between Renato and Heather. Renato was softly clapping his hands, repeating, "No worries, girls, . . . Don't worry . . . Don't worry." Then, "Why didn't I just take Hugh's car?" and then, "I can't believe I have no car right now!" and then, "I've got a beautiful car in Savannah."

"Ren?" Mae started, looking straight ahead at nothing. "I need to ask you something, and you better tell me the truth."

"Yeah?"

"You gonna tell me the truth?"

"Probably not. I don't know."

"Renato Reyes-Sanchez," Mae paused for a moment. Renato and Heather both stared at her and waited. "Are you my father?"

"What is wrong with you? No, Mae! Hugh's your dad - what- why would you think I'd be your daddy?" Renato laughed loudly for the first time since Hugh was shot.

"Because you acting so nervous about going to see Momma! Like you can't wait to see her, wondering, 'Will she like me?' and because you act like you hate her so much, and I think you act that way because you and Momma are secretly in love and you have to tell us something: 'I'm your father, girls.'" Mae threw her voice low, and Renato stared at her and smiled.

"You're a first-class nut, you know it?" Renato answered. "I'm gonna ask the next bus if they have a nut section where you can sit."

"So, you're not? I'm wrong?"

"Mae! I am not — thank God above! - I am not your daddy!" He paused to notice her response.

"Then what are you so nervous about?"

"Nothing," he was lying. Heather sensed it when he jerked his head as if in discomfort; he was lying about something. "I guess I'm just nervous about being responsible for two lovely girls without Hugh here."

"Renato, you're not responsible for me. And I can take care of my sister," Heather said. If Renato planned on dumping the girls, Heather needed to be ready.

Renato studied her for a moment and said, "I know you can, Heather. I know you're grown, and I'm probably wasting my time."

Mae looked at Heather with her mouth resting open like she witnessed a tragedy. She said to Renato, "If you're my real father, Renato, goodness! Just tell me! The thought makes me feel like I'm gonna throw up, and just let me get this out of my stomach."

"Mae, you're stupid," Heather told her. "He's not old enough. Momma's much older than Renato. He's not much older than me." Heather wondered if he heard her. It didn't matter; she wasn't talking to him.

They rested on the station bench by the road, vulnerable to the next moment. Heather could part ways here, but they were probably stronger together for now.

Heather looked down the road every few minutes, but it turned into a black canvas, until headlights beamed from a distance, shining and pointing towards them, coming closer.

15

The Hawks

truck passed slowly and stopped on the other side of the bus station. It parked at an imposing enough distance. A tall man got out and swung his arms like a pendulum, unloading bags and crates from his truck bed, turning to study Renato, Heather, and Mae from time to time. He wore overalls comfortably over his long legs as if the two of them were a life-long match. Once his truck was emptied, he walked towards them, staring. They sat motionless and stared in response.

"You sleeping on this bench tonight?" the man asked. His long face was compatible with the rest of his body. If he smiled, he would have looked kind.

"I don't know what we're going to do yet," Renato answered.

"We're headed for New York," Mae interrupted, "New York City!" The man raised his brow in surprise and noticed

Renato and Heather's excitement didn't match Mae's. Renato slightly shook his head to the man.

The man's hands sandwiched his thin waist and rested. He spoke to Renato, "So, you're trying to get home to your wife?" The man's eyes covered every inch of space down the road and in the vicinity of the station.

"No sir, not married," Renato answered.

The man glanced at the girls and then Renato, "Prostitutes?"

"What? No!"

"Your slave girls?" the man tried again, standing still over them.

Heather found this guess more plausible than being mistaken for a prostitute.

"What the- no! Can I help you, mister?"

The man held out his hands, "Just asking, if you need help. Are you in trouble? I don't want trouble in my house," the man hesitated and then added, "I got room for you and the girls to sleep tonight, just for tonight; but it's in Oglesby, so it's a long ride," he motioned for them to jump in the bed of his truck. Renato froze for a second and then perked his back straight up. The man glared at them as they continued sitting still and added, "We do this from time to time, my wife and I. Offer bus passengers stuck on the bench somewhere's to sleep." He walked towards his truck and turned around to say, "Might not be the direction you want."

"Girls, let's go," Renato said. He stood up quickly and gravitated toward the truck. Following Renato's every step was not normal; Heather didn't like it. How was she supposed to be okay with climbing into some strange white man's truck, standing there in overalls he had worn all his life, after he deemed Mae and her to be prostitutes and slaves? Heather replayed the evening, looking for reason: they were eating in a fine restaurant two hours ago. Mrs. Whitney had to go home. She was nervous when she left, and then she was gone. Just the remnants of Renato, whose fidgeting made little sense. Now, Mae and Renato were climbing into a truck bed. Who was there to stop Heather and tell her how stupid this was?

"Renato," Heather's voice fluttered as she stood at the back of the truck leaning on one leg like she was comfortable with the situation, "I believe me and Mae will find our way back on our own."

"Your way back where, Heather?" Renato asked. He was already seated in the truck with Mae.

"Home. Sterling," Heather hated saying it. She was giving up.

"Sterling isn't really home anymore, Heather. . . But, you know what? You're a grown woman. You do whatever you think is best."

'Mae, get off the truck," Heather snapped, bitterly angry. The man cranked the motor.

"No, Heather! You heard Ren. Sterling's not home. New York is!" She sounded like she had a microphone as she tried to resound over the motor. "We're on our way!" Mae squealed, standing in the truck bed. She smiled down at Renato and shimmied down close beside him with her legs stretched straight out. The truck engine rumbled loudly and interrupted Heather's thoughts.

Heather had a new authority in her life. Mae was a

responsibility to be led, not followed. When did this responsibility become Heather's authority? Heather faced the new revelation of who she was — a follower. Her responsibilities, her leaders, she followed both, and Heather followed Mae. She climbed in the truck bed and avoided seeing Renato's or Mae's eyes mocking her. She sat on the other side of Renato and felt embarrassed. They rested against the cabin of the truck to block as much wind as possible. The frosty air relieved Heather's hot cheeks. She hated New York. She hated Renato, and Mae annoyed her. She should have left Mae with Renato, since they wanted to go so badly. The man gave them two scratchy wool blankets that provided little warmth. Renato sat between the sisters and placed his arms around both of them. *Wings of shelter, he probably thinks!* Heather kept her body stiff. The truck drove through the dark, and black surrounded them. The motor was loud, and the wind bit them relentlessly. Heather understood the anger in the cold, and it cooled her as if saying, *I know!* Leaning in on Renato was inevitable to sit comfortably. They passed a field of soybean bushels, the rows of crop bushels were a cream light by the starry sky, just by the road. The rows quickly darkened, sucked into the night.

"Your granddad used to say those rows looked like piano keys," Renato said, "He'd say that's where God played music, why the field hands were always singing." The last thing Heather wanted to hear was another story of oppression. She needed no reminder that submission ran through her Negro veins.

"Renato," Heather asked, "where's Oglesby?" Renato stared at her for a couple of seconds, so close to her face she could have kissed him again — or spit in his face.

"Heather," he said, "we're going south. Right now." He smiled. Heather was closer to her dream, to her future husband, to the ground where Hugh grew up.

"Ren, I'm freezin!" Mae blared. "Get me outta here!" She bundled in the blanket.

Heather still wasn't comfortable enough to smile and be friends, but hope grew, finally. She tried to overcome her aching frigid body with this hope, but she cried. Mae didn't know where Oglesby was, or she would have spoken. She noticed Heather crying, and buried her own face to cry, too. She may have been crying loudly, but the motor drowned her voice. Mae looked up to connect eyes with Heather, and the reproach of the last few days flooded back into Heather's chest and spread to her fingers. The cold and miserable truck bed comforted their teared-soaked souls, understanding them. The air grew dark before the day should have been over.

After an hour, the truck turned onto a dirt path that stretched up a hill to a two-story farmhouse, the man's home. His land was thick in grass but empty. His house stood tall and alone in the middle of the vast, void property aligned with eerie trees, swaying earnestly, not daring to come any closer. The strong wind felt nice despite the rolling clouds and the diagonal trees trying to intimidate the guests and warn them. The upstairs windows were dark, and one corner of the downstairs shined a yellow light out onto the wrap-around porch's corner. The truck turned off, and the loving silence closed a chapter. They felt like they were born again, ready to step even closer to dying.

The man opened the tail gate. They followed the man into the house toward the lights and stopped right inside the door. A small woman of about 60 carried a lantern and paused from walked quickly to them and stared at them. She wore a handkerchief in her peppered hair, and her face was perfectly oval. Her pudgy nose was an unfortunate distraction; she had a boring face, with an expression like she knew it but pretended she didn't think so.

"Hi, how are you? You all?" she asked with concerned eyes and a plastic smile revealing perfectly symmetrical lips and teeth. She stood at the entryway, blocking their ability to walk any further into the house. The wind was whistling behind them. She looked up at her husband like he was the only one that understood her question. Mae tried to imitate the lady's smile with big eyes.

"They got kicked off the bus on account of the colored girls. We'll put 'em up tonight and send 'em out come morning," the man told her. Rain slowly splatted on their tin roof. The man picked up a second lantern from a wooden meal table. Another lantern shone brightly from the kitchen counter. They didn't have electric power yet. Hugh told Heather how Sterling was fortunate to have it; Heather didn't really believe him, thinking he was just wanting her to be grateful for something. The only reason anybody in Sterling had electric power rested solely on the Whitneys.

"Are they working for us now?" the boring-faced lady asked her husband.

He shifted his feet and answered assertively, "No, they need a place for the night." Behind the lady, a large banner attached to a stick leaned against the wall. It read "Vote Dry!

Anti-Saloon League" in large letters. She stood blocking Renato and the sisters from coming past the doorway.

"Oh, I see," she responded. "Well, for free?"

An awkward few seconds of silence prompted her to look at them for an answer.

"Ma'am, I don't intend taking anything from you or your family," Heather spoke up. However, this was not entirely true; Heather's eyes had already scanned the kitchen to the right and located a stack of tin cups and tin plates, a ladle, a scoop paddle, a kettle, a food grater, a wooden box— *What's in there?* — and a bowl of apples. Apples evoke inescapable temptation. The family room was to their right. Heather noticed candelabras with white candles and black wicks on each side of a mantle, a large book Heather believed to be the Bible centered on a table set beside the sofa; a dark-colored vase, undoubtedly fragile. The spacious room looked empty, and Heather's eyes returned to the bowl of apples. "No ma'am; not for free," Heather ascertained.

Renato added, "No ma'am. I can pay you for all your . . . hospitality. We're . . . grateful." He took off his hat as he spoke. The tempo of the rain quickened on the tin roof and rose to a haunting roar.

The lady's smile vanished and she stared at Renato. "Are you homeless?" She increased her volume over the violence above their heads.

"No ma'am," Renato shouted back, glancing up at the roof and out the windows. "We still have our homes. In Sterling." With this, the lady showed how she had perfected the closed smile while her eyes remained stoic and shifting.

"Well," she paused, stepped back, and guided them to her

kitchen table. "Have some bread . . . and water. Little girl, do you like water?" she asked Mae.

Mae sat at the table and looked up at her, then at Renato. "Ren, why are we here?" Her voice muffled with the marching rain. "We gotta' get to New York." She looked back up at the lady. "Yes ma'am, I do drink water." Heather sat across from Mae, close to the bowl of small apples. She hoped they'd be offered to them.

"Oh!" the lady placed her hand on her chest. "Then get up and help me. You shan't just sit there!" Mae turned to Renato with large, surprised eyes. The tall husband in overalls strode long steps of routine in and out of the kitchen. Mae stood and followed the lady around the table to a large tin bucket. The lady gave Mae a large ladle and a tin cup. A sink with a faucet sat dry and unused.

"We'll need to go out and pump the water when the rain subsides," she said.

"I'm so . . . happy . . . to help you, Mrs...," Renato walked toward the counter where the lady stood by a third lighted lantern. Heather could take one of the apples and slip it in the pocket of her dress.

"Mrs. Hawk. Mr. And Mrs. Hawk," she answered with a wry smile, "He's Ralph and I'm Elma." She widened her smile — a flirtatious smile? Mrs. Hawk leaned against her counter, wiping her tiny hands on her apron, smiling at Renato. Renato stared back at her and stood a five-foot distance in front of her leaning on the counter.

Two apples would fit fine in Heather's pocket.

Renato was flirting with this poor old farm wife. A shake of thunder outdoors snapped them out of their nonsense.

"Actually, why don't you sit down and let us serve you?" Renato suggested. Mrs. Hawk shied her face with a little giggle. The tin roof echoes became more bearable than the cumbrous kitchen engagement.

"No sir! You're my guest. This is the least I can do."

Heather almost asked for an apple.

"Ren, I'm tired," Mae interrupted the uncomfortable moment.

They managed through a little bread and water before they were led to a back-corner sun porch with a sofa, a cushioned church pew, and some wooden chairs set in the long, narrow space. The Hawk couple left them with a lantern and rules to not leave the sun porch unless they were leaving the house. Mr. and Mrs. Hawk departed upstairs, and Heather helped herself to the apples. She was able to fit five small apples in her pockets. Mae uncovered a pile of blankets in a closet. Everyone settled in the sun porch for the night.

Rain pounded and tapped on the tin roof like a cadence, until Mae spoke up. The inevitable question came again.

"When will we be in New York with Momma?"

Renato plopped down on the floor and leaned against the wall behind a wooden end table. He dimmed the lantern light. On the other side of the end table was the long church bench where Mae sat under a blanket, perked up staring at Renato. Renato grabbed a flask out of his bag, swallowed a swig, took off his hat, and covered his face with it.

"You ignoring me, Renato?" Mae asked. A cacophony of thunder and lightning followed Mae's question. The house shook in the battlefield and startled the three guests. They looked out the large windows lighting up like opened eyelids.

Mae, finding no awe in the power of nature, turned back to Renato.

"When, Ren?" she asked.

"Mae- . . . get some sleep," he answered. The thunder and lightning continued. The house creaked and the wind groaned like a devil. "Sounds like a tornado," Renato said under the hat. The girls expected lightning to light up the outdoors again any second.

"Stop changing the subject! I can see the storm! I don't care!" A low moan of thunder shook the house; she insisted, "New York – when Renato? Just tell me." Heather lay still, waiting to hear Renato's response.

"Mae!" Renato sat up and breathed in before continuing, "We're . . ." He stopped and looked at Heather, both bewildered as to why they were lying to Mae.

"Mae," Heather started, "we're not going just yet."

"Wait, . . . what? Why not? Where . . . where we going?" Mae looked at Heather with her head lowered as if she was about to curse her.

"Mae, we"- Renato tried again, but Heather again intervened.

"We're headed south, Mae. Back to our roots, you know. Just first, Mae," Heather poured out the words like she was putting out a fire, "and if you don't like it, then we'll go, okay? We'll go to New York. And if Momma wants to find us, she can."

Mae looked at Renato and then Heather, "You lied to me. You both did." Mae spoke through clinched teeth, snapped her blanket off, and stood up. "You're taking me to New York, Renato," she raised her voice, "You're taking me, Renato! . . .

Heather?"

"Mae," started Renato. He sat up. "Look, Mae. . . Listen. . . Mae, I couldn't let you leave with her- with your Ma. She's not planning anything good, Mae."

"Momma don't know? You stole me! You stole me!" Mae shouted from her angry belly.

"No, Mae," Renato answered, slowly standing. "Listen, I gotta take care of you and Heather, and we're heading down to Georgia." It was said.

"No. No. No, we're not, Renato!" Mae stomped her foot. "We're going home, and to New York!" Mae's voice increased with each word. Heather shushed her.

"He's stealing us!" Mae boomed out.

The Hawk couple's footsteps preceded their appearance at the wide doorway of the sunroom. The storm slowly settled and quieted down as if it wanted to hear the indoor storm.

"Shut up, Mae!" Heather demanded as curtly as she could as she sat up. She turned to the couple and exclaimed, "No, he didn't!"

"Is that alcohol in my home!" Mrs. Hawk exclaimed, staring at the flask in Renato's hand. "It's illegal in our country, and it's not allowed in our house!"

"Yes, he did bring it! Took us from our Momma, too!" They shouted at each other at the same time, a shouting mess, and Renato stayed quiet and slipped the flask back in his bag. He slowly reached for his shoes. Heather noticed and placed her feet on the floor.

"He's kidnapped us!" Mae shouted, staring at the Hawks.

"No. No, Mae. No, Mr. Hawk," Renato stood to face Mr. Hawk. "I just can't get them home tonight. I'm a friend."

"I'm calling the police," Mr. Hawk answered.

Within the same space and time allotted for the single thought of Mr. Hawk's words, Renato pulled out a gun and pointed it at Mr. Hawk.

"No, you're not," Renato calmly answered. "Girls, pack up. We're leaving." Renato commanded the couple to sit on the couch in the sun porch, and he politely asked Mrs. Hawk to pack his things around the couch into his travel bag.

Heather saw this same thing last week. A gun pointed at a poor man's head. The man didn't do anything wrong. Shots were coming. One at Hugh's head. He looked a little mean at Heather when she spoke up before he got shot, she remembered. She knew he didn't want his killer to kill her, too.

Why did Renato pull out a gun? The Hawks sat still, afraid to move, with their mouths opened, eyes big, and brows in fervent worry. Renato was the one who told Heather to trust him.

The same terror surfaced to Heather's skin and constricted her throat. She tried to shout *Stop!* but it came out silently.

Renato mumbled, "Girls, hurry up and get out the front door. . . . Keep going . . . Hurry up." He kept the gun pointed at the petrified Hawks sitting on the couch. What was he doing with a gun? The couple held their helpless hands up, just as Hugh had done. Heather felt dizzy but picked up her feet. Mae stood still, changing her composure from defiance to fright. She then quickly gathered everything and shuffled to the door. Heather followed her somehow in her daze.

They hurried out the front door quickly and without speaking. Heather stood on the front porch in the dark and listened to the inside conversation.

"Girls, go!" hollered Renato, but they didn't. "See, Mr. Hawk, I can't sleep here if you're making threats about the police. Ma'am, I'll take my bag." Renato opened the screen door and joined Heather and Mae on the porch. "Girls, run!" Mae's flight instincts leaped her off the steps of the porch and down the hill into the darkness. Heather stood and watched her as Renato rushed down the steps. He turned around to Heather.

"Heather, my God, you gotta run! Run!" he shouted.

"Heather, come on!" Mae bolted in desperation from the darkness. Heather sprinted down past Renato. The downhill slope caused her feet to tumble, and she fell in the soaked grass. Renato grabbed her up.

"Please, just run, Heather," Renato strained out. The three of them kept going down the dark, wet grassy lawn. The storm remnants in the air soaked their faces. The road was soon visible in the darkness, and they were almost to it. A shotgun blasted from the farmhouse front porch. The bullet smeared through the air between the heads of Mae and Renato. Renato ducked and then looked behind him, as they all did. Mr. Hawk stood on his front porch with a shotgun rifle. Heather felt like her blood froze, and she screamed.

"Heather, just run. Just keep running to the right of the road, now," Renato said just before another gunshot. "Girls, keep running!" They pounded their feet on the wet dirt road. Pools of puddles, mush of mud. Heather felt the splashes of wet dirt flying between the ground and her knees. Eventually, they were out of the reach of the Hawks' residence and from bullets blasted from their front porch.

They gasped for air and stamped on the gravel dirt road in darkness. The silhouettes of tall trees were barely distinct against the black sky. Panting in the middle of the cold road, Heather stopped.

"What are you doing with a gun?" Heather demanded.

"Heather, I wasn't gonna shoot them."

"Why would you need to? Why do you care if Mr. Hawk calls the police?" Heather exhaled out the words between gasps of breath.

"Can I shoot it?" Mae asked.

"No."

"Why not?"

"You'll shoot me," Renato answered.

"What's going on?" Heather demanded.

"We need to keep walking. He may be chasing us," Renato said. They ran and panted in fear down the road.

"Renato!" Heather demanded again. They kept walking at a fast pace. "I'm going back. This was all a bad idea. I should've never got on that truck. I knew better. Daddy'd be so mad about that." Heather turned around to walk back towards the Hawk's. She was fine at home in Sterling, living beside Mrs. Whitney, and working at the store. Maybe she'd see Savannah another day, but no time soon.

"Okay," Renato stopped and answered, "and I'm sorry about the gun."

They stood still.

"See ya, Ren," Mae trotted past Renato towards Heather.

"What are you going to do?" Heather asked Renato, pulling her blanket around her tighter.

"I'm going home to Savannah. I got nowhere else to go,"

Renato answered. Heather thought of Sterling and the two hours to get there. She stood still and stared at Renato. Trees dropped and plopped raindrops to the ground in a fuss over the storm that just tore through.

"Come on, Heather," Mae said.

"Mae, . . . we can't. We can't get home tonight. We gotta stay with Ren a little while longer." She took a step closer to Renato.

"Then I'll go myself!" Mae began in the opposite direction, holding her blanket around her. Renato moaned some incomprehensible Spanish with his hands out toward the sky.

"Mae, stop! You're staying with me, Mae!" Heather hollered and grabbed Mae's arm. "You're with me!" Heather exclaimed as if she now realized this new journey.

Mae followed Heather, and Heather followed Renato.

They walked together in the dark. Mae and Heather's legs shivered. Their feet were wet in their shoes. They kept the Hawks' blankets around them as they stumbled down the dark gravel dirt road.

They walked on in silence down the black eerie road.

"Stay close," Renato told the girls.

16

A Separate Walk

They dodged bullets from Mr. Hawk, and if they weren't depleted from air and gasping, and if they weren't moist with sweat and used raindrops, and if they didn't have mud in their wet socks that didn't help the feelings of nausea, they would have felt invincible.

They walked in the middle of the old roadbed in the darkness for a long moment without speaking.

"Heather, why'd you lie to me?" Mae asked.

Heather said nothing.

"Alright," Renato sounded irritated. "Mae, I'm sorry I didn't tell you, okay? But Mae," he let out a groan of frustration. The bliss of being free from bullet holes was done.

"I'm not going South, Heather," Mae said. No one cared to respond.

A tractor port with a low roof sat a few yards back from the road, a good 300 yards from the Hawk's farmhouse, most likely belonging to the Hawk's. A path connected the building to the road. The building opened to the outdoors on one side, which was helpful under the pitch-black sky. A plowing tractor and a car were parked inside. Deeper into the building was darkness. Leftover raindrops fell and patted in continuity around the building. Renato lit a match to reveal two wooden worktables and a spread of metal tools and contraptions. The ground halfway in was dark with storm water, and the two vehicles were beaded from the heavy rain. Renato blew out his light.

"We can sleep inside the car I guess, for tonight, for a few hours," Renato suggested.

For a moment they stared at each other with a sore humility. They were homeless on this night, more homeless than Hooverville folks. Mae and Heather stood still. They tried to soak in the truth of the situation as they felt cold and dampness seep through to their leg bones. Renato peered in the car and pulled on the handle. It opened, and he scrunched his shoulders as if startled.

"Can't we just take this car?" Mae asked.

"There's no key," answered Renato. He opened the car door wide, and Mae climbed through, lying down and taking up the small backseat space.

"I'm going home tomorrow," Mae said. Renato closed the door and turned to Heather.

"You sitting up front with me?" Renato entered in at the driver's seat. Heather had no other door to open except the passenger's side door. She scooted in beside Renato without looking at him for several seconds. The car was cold. With a placid expression, Renato opened his arms and hands, inviting Heather to be held. His sleeves were still rolled up, and a melancholic sense washed through Heather. She remembered her father. She sat upright with intentional space from Renato until her eyes closed.

When she opened her eyes, she saw the outdoors through the front windshield of the car. The sun had not yet risen as the air was still gray. They all unfolded and awoke. The outline of the Hawks' driveway cut through the rolling yard. They were too close. They quickly exited the car, scurried to the right, down the road.

"Wait, I'm going back to the Hawk's to get a ride back home. You don't need to come," Mae said. "I don't want you to." She turned to stroll the other way.

"Mae, you gonna get Ren in trouble," Heather scratched out of her sleepy throat. Heather's face felt like it was still trying to wake up as her feet carried it along. The three of them had morning puff in their faces. Mae and Heather kept the Hawks' blankets around them.

They heard a front door slam, and they could see Mr. Hawk standing on his front porch. He was looking back at them.

"The police are on their way," he shouted. "You're all three going to jail, so don't move!" He had a rifle in his hands, and he walked down the porch steps.

"I ain't going to jail," Mae said, and then she shouted at Mr. Hawk, "I didn't do nothing!" She stood still.

"Mae, let's go!"

"No!" Mr. Hawk was walking towards them.

"Mae, he'll shoot us!"

"But what about Momma -- I wanna go to New York!" She turned her head from Heather back to Mr. Hawk. Mr. Hawk stopped and aimed his rifle towards them.

They bolted down the road.

After a couple of minutes, Renato said, "Alright girls, slow down. I think we're out of harm's way."

They stood panting again, too tired to talk about the law, Mr. Hawk, or Mae's dreams.

"Let's just hide when we hear a car," Renato told them.

"I have apples," Heather managed in an exhale.

They walked and crunched their apples. Walking was a growing norm in the country. Unless the Hawk's themselves drove by, they looked like anyone else. They passed three walkers heading north. None of them cared to speak.

Only two cars passed them all day. Never a police officer.

They journeyed at a golden dawn, cold and breezy, an unkind welcome. Small knolls and meadows of grass on both sides of them showed a bigger sky. Dark teal speckled orange on their left and dimmed quickly to a black sky to their right. That's how Heather knew they were walking south, towards her dream, her new home, her Negro man. She almost forgot about going back to Sterling, except for watching Mae stepping further away from her own dream.

"Mae, why do you wanna go to New York?" Heather asked.

"To be with Momma, like she told us to," Mae answered with obvious passion.

"She don't wanna be with you," Renato offered.

"Shut up, Ren!" Mae answered.

"She don't," Renato said.

"I need a momma, and she's mine." The argument whirled in a circle, as it always did.

Heather wanted to enjoy the walk, every step, closer to

what she always loved. She lagged a bit behind Renato and Mae. She figured the only way to know who and what she truly loved was to take a step forward and see where her toes pointed. Hers were pointing south. *My man's ahead. My Black, sweaty, angel of a man.*

Mae had a fantasy, not a dream. Heather told her so.

"So's yours, Heather," Mae sighed and spoke through her teeth. "You're headed towards cotton fields, Negro."

Heather tuned Mae out and stared at the back of Renato's head as she walked behind him. Hugh's fedora was slightly too big for him. He wore his dark brown wool coat over his blazer, and he carried a bag of belongings with a drawstring over his shoulder. He looked like anybody else from behind. Nothing special like Lilac or Veronica believed. Except he carried a gun.

"Why didn't you pull out your gun and shoot Daddy's killer?" Heather demanded.

"I didn't have it with me," Renato looked to the side to speak as he walked. "Hugh wouldn't let me bring it to work." He kept walking south, and Heather and Mae kept following him.

"Did you shoot Daddy's killer, Ren?" Heather asked. Palpable contention wrinkled everyone's eyebrows, and nature's golden, joyful air couldn't overpower it.

Renato stopped to turn around. "How? I was laid out half-dead in bed. I did not, Heather." He stared at her and slumped his neck again, which she now realized had been up this morning. She stopped and stared as placidly as he. He added, "I didn't kill nobody. I told you that, didn't I?"

They commenced walking. The road was mostly dirt with

loose gravel, spaced out around water puddles reflecting the tall, dense trees walled on each side of the road.

Renato turned around again to speak. "If you girls don't wanna go with me, it's fine. I probably won't make it down there before getting shot anyway." He stopped and said, "But your daddy wouldn't like me leaving you — you know that — and I am going to try . . . to stay with you . . . to do this for Hugh."

"Okay, Ren," Mae answered, and they walked.

"My apologies, Ren. Tying you down to honor Daddy," Heather said.

Where did this noble character come from? Wasn't he cornered? Blackmailed? Heather's thoughts swarmed like black birds in her head.

"Well, you sure as hell don't make it easy, Heather," Renato answered.

Heather wasn't sure she and Mae would go South; she was ambiguous on disregarding her sister's dream for New York, for a mother. Heather used to wish for a mother, too; perhaps this was why Heather disregarded Mae's dream.

The sky was still, compared to the night before, and transformed into a bright blue. They grew used to walking in wet shoes. The air was crisp and tolerable. Peaceful. Peace is more obvious after a long period of not having it, no matter how short-lived.

Mae's breathing quickened into huffs. She cried. Heather said nothing and let her. Mae's walk progressed to a stomp, but she kept going. She stared straight ahead with pursed lips. Heather and Renato walked in silence for quite a while, in ode to Mae.

"Renato," Mae began. The only other noise was the rumbling, scratchy gravel rocks under their shoes.

"Yeah, Mae?"

"When you were asleep, after you got shot, I walked in your bedroom one day, and I saw Heather sucking on your lips, kissing you hard."

That little brat. Heather thought. The next few seconds surfaced Heather's heartbeat to her throat. The best thing that could have happened was for Renato to ignore her and keep walking. Laugh it off and forget it. But he didn't. He stopped, stared dumbfounded at Mae for a second, and turned his head and stared at Heather. If any automobile, animal, bird, walker, or wind wanted to come down the road, it must have stopped, too.

"What?" was all he said, staring straight at Heather. She didn't know how she was supposed to answer the question – *what it was? What it felt like? What I was thinking? What happened? What his lips tasted like?* Heather stopped walking, too. She stood as strong as she could fabricate in the middle of the road and stared back with a fake dignity.

"What do you mean 'what'? I kissed you, just like Mae said!" Her voice cracked before she finished. She continued staring at him. She lifted her chin a bit higher, and he kept staring at her. She could have stared all day because she was petrified, and that was hard to mask. Heather could see the amusement behind the artificial stern face that Renato tried to show her. Fortunately, Mae broke the staring force.

"I did, too, Renato. I kissed you right on your lips." His mouth opened in astonishment as he stared dumbfounded at Mae, releasing Heather's imprisonment.

"So . . . the two of you played with my lifeless body like a toy, huh? Anything else I should know? Did you look under the covers to see anything else, huh? . . . Huh, girls?"

"Please stop calling me a girl," Heather answered curtly. She was called a girl for the last time, and she had to defend herself with something. "I am a woman, and believe me, Renato," she dared, "I kissed you like a woman. And no, . . . I'm also a lady with class. Don't you accuse me of-of . . . looking at your private parts without your permission!" With this Mae let out a healthy laugh full of glee, which was good. Renato fueled her laughter and spoke again.

"Without my permission?" Renato found a place to poke fun as Mae wailed in laughter. "Well, I'm sorry, Heather. I couldn't give you permission. I was half-dead!" He joined Mae in merriment. "Did you try to ask me, by chance?" They ambled on. Mae looked a little happier. Heather followed the two of them, keeping space.

Although embarrassed, Heather was relieved he now knew the truth, but for some reason she felt like there was some unfinished business, like she owed him, like she deserved payback. Maybe he would sneak a kiss in return. It sounded silly in her head, and she scolded herself for her thoughts.

He didn't mention it again.

The worn-out gravel road stretched moist and gray with dips filled with black water puddles. It curled in hills so they couldn't see too far up ahead. The sky brightened and the sun rose from the left of them. They walked a while. They were hungry and thirsty. Heather endured, figuring they'd arrive in Savannah in a day or two.

She also hoped the road would arrive at a town where they could find transportation, but no signs of human life were seen for most of the day. They stopped and rested a few times. They took off their shoes, socks, and stockings to rest their throbbing feet, and then they had no choice but to keep walking. On they traveled as the gravel road transcended into brown dirt.

"Shut up, Heather," Renato broke the silence. Mae turned to look at Heather and back to Renato.

With a smile, Mae said, "She didn't say anything, Ren!"

"She's thinking too loudly," Renato answered.

The road lay between a dense forest on each side of them, with trees standing in allegiance as if they'd been expecting them. The trees sometimes stepped aside to offer a field blanketed with treasure — wheat, crops, even unruly grass. And a tired old baby blue sky sheltered them. *Daddy would love this scenery.* Heather thought. She pretended he was beside her, looking around, smiling. Once the sky's warmth covered their faces, the trees stepped back forward, and they were again cradled on a cool shaded path. The walk was peaceful, no room for weariness or fear, but a great deal lonesome.

In the late afternoon, the sound of voices at a far distance was a precious melody. They saw nothing for almost a mile later, as the voices rang clearer.

To their left, the land slowly ascended, and a large, two-story barn —larger than any barn Heather thought existed, especially back in Sterling— echoed the voices they heard. Behind the barn, on up the hill, was a farmhouse and some small sheds standing scattered in between. Plush farmed fields of green surrounded the barn. Strange sight, a farming family that didn't appear to have suffered as most farming families they knew. Several people —too many to have lived there— strolled in and out of the barn. Some carried crates and pulled horses. Many congregated in small groups, and many more loafed around aimlessly. Renato left the path and walked towards the barn in curiosity. Heather and Mae followed. As they approached the barn, Heather noticed these visitors looked as tired as she did.

17

Within a Storm

A tornado rummaged through the night before, south of this plantation that Renato, Heather, and Mae now stared at. The owners of the plantation extended an invitation to neighbors who suffered from the storm. Renato, Heather, and Mae were on the northern outskirts of the funnel on the Hawks' property.

They walked up the hill with long faces, panting breaths, dusty clothes with splatters of caked mud, and they walked as slow as everyone else.

The double barn doors were shaped in an arch about 20 feet high and were propped open. Renato, Mae, and Heather paused at the entrance. Inside, horses were shut in stables, and haystacks served as seats. The center made an open circle. Nests of hay aligned the wall where people lay and slept. Long wooden tables were lined up and placed in the center of the barn holding buckets of water, scattered food, and a few blankets. Several people were eating soup and bread. The high ceilings made the barn seem wider than it was. Sunlight streamed in from the opened doors. All the strange faces inside were scurrying around, serving one another. A few paused to see the newest visitors. Heather shifted her eyes throughout the barn, breathing faintly, hoping not to be noticed. Even Renato wasn't white. Taking another step was like chancing a land mine. Maybe the whole crowd wouldn't arm against them, but one voice in opposition would crumble Heather. Embarrass her. Degrade her. She looked at Renato for reassurance, and his eyes were wide with uncertainty, and his head and neck slumped over. They were too tired to turn on any charismatic qualities. It was a vulnerable walk. Heather felt like everyone around stared at them. As they moved closer to the center, Renato placed his arm around Heather. It was a compassion she hadn't received since Hugh's own arms hugged her, encouraging her to keep hoping. Mae stared at the horses with grand admiration, noticing nothing else.

They weren't turned away. A woman in a long skirt met eyes with them and pointed to a space on the far-right side where a haystack and a nest of hay sat ready to be claimed. Everyone had something more on their minds. No one asked them to leave. Apparently, they looked like victims of the cyclone, not a completely inaccurate assessment.

Renato led Mae and Heather to sit on the haystack as he stood in line to get them some soup and bread. Renato came back with two bowls of hot potato soup. The families were careful with portions, understandably. Ultimately, they gave what they could. Heather envied that kind of grace, a softer kind, she believed. Renato, Mae, and Heather filled their stomachs with enough, and Heather found a place to rest her head against the haystack.

She felt like she had only blinked, but when she opened her eyes, golden morning light trickled inside the barn full of sleeping people, or people quietly coming in and out. A new day, again already. Heather cuddled beside Mae. As soon as Mae awoke, she stood and walked to a stable door.

"Saint William, . . . good morning, sweet honey!" Mae looked up at a massive brown horse and pet the sides of its face. She hugged its neck and continued speaking lovingly to the animal, swaying side to side, anchored by her chubby legs. Heather stayed still, fearing any movement could disrupt the calm and uninterrupted. She tried to relax; she leaned against the haystack and admired the silence of the barn's grand space. Other colored folks were there, too. That helped.

Heather heard a familiar voice.

"Mae found a new friend last night," Veronica Nolan said, standing behind Heather, smiling.

What is Veronica doing here? Heather stared at her, dumbfounded. Veronica's blond hair was freshly washed, and she wore a bright blue clean dress. It looked like she just starched it. Her beige skin was clean and supple. "The owners let her feed and brush Saint William. She begged them to let her sleep in there with it, but they told her no," Veronica smiled, "The people here are good people. They're friends of mine."

"What are you—?"

"I'm here to help out," Veronica answered and sat on a haystack next to Heather's straw bed. Heather noticed how

Veronica wouldn't turn her head. "The tornado wiped out a whole town south of here. The whole town's gone! The Palmers own this place. They were spared. They're rich, and they're helping."

Renato walked towards the two ladies, and Veronica stood up. Renato stood next to Veronica, facing Heather; and since Heather couldn't hide her disgust, she climbed to her feet and ventured over to Mae.

"Mornin', Liar," Mae greeted Heather. Mae wore a thick white cardigan sweater given to her by a tornado victim the evening before. Her insult bothered Heather no more than what already nagged at her. Why was Veronica Nolan there? Veronica pranced beside Heather just as Heather was waking, as her hair was unformed and her face puffy. Even her mind was not awake enough to gather any poise. Heather cut her eyes at Mae and glared at her. She needed to unload her irritable burden somewhere, and Mae was there.

"Mae . . ." Heather began, not knowing what anger she was to pour out, "you ever wish someone was out of the way, as in dead, or gone, at the least, so that you could live your life?" She leaned against the fence and stared at Saint William standing still pretending he wasn't listening to their conversation. "People that get in my way, if they'd go a different way, away from me."

"You wish I was dead?" Mae asked. She stood in the stall with the horse, acting as if this wasn't her first time.

"No, never," Heather answered.

Life could have been better if things were different, always. Heather guessed that's what life was, something never as good as something else. Even for Saint William.

"Why are you and Renato keeping me and Momma apart?" Mae asked.

"I don't know," Heather answered, giving a partial lie.

"Heather, Renato hates Momma." Mae brushed the horse on its back. Heather finally took a long stare at Saint William. What a beautiful creature. So docile. He could stomp and crush Mae, but he submitted to her and accepted the flood of affection from this stranger.

"He seems to like *us*," Heather replied as she watched Mae brush the horse. "Maybe love us?"

"This horse don't love you," Mae answered.

"I'm talking about Ren, Mae."

Mae kept brushing the horse. "He hates Momma more than he loves us." Mae was probably right. She paused from brushing Saint William.

"Do you think he'd shoot Momma?" Mae asked. Good question.

"Heather, we need to talk," Renato said, standing behind Heather.

"Okay, but can we eat first?" Heather requested as she turned towards him. A group of women sat large steaming pots on the wooden tables with tin cups in a sack.

Mae glared at Renato as if she had to protect her horse.

"What do you want?" Mae insisted.

"Nothing, Mae. . . Beautiful horse!"

"He loves me," Mae said. "He stares at me like I'm the most beautiful woman in the world." She spoke with a bruised enthusiasm, glaring at Renato and standing firm in front of Saint William.

"And a smart horse."

She showed no appreciation for his flattery. "I'm going to ride him up to New York City. He's a racehorse, so he can get me there a whole lot faster than you can."

"That's true. Can we eat, Mae?" Renato replied as if irked. Mae lifted her eyebrows and her head, and she primped around Renato to the food. He humbly followed her. Startled again this morning, Heather stopped to see Veronica stomping toward them from outside the back doors frantically.

"Grab some food and come outside. Quickly!" she quietly commanded them. She helped get their oats and scooted them outside to a forlorn fire pit, blazing for no one. The morning was bright with a blue sky, as if asking for forgiveness for its previous behavior. The air was chilly. They gathered around the fire's warmth.

"Anywhere I can clean up a bit?" Renato asked.

"They have a wash bin of hot water right inside the shed. But you'll need to move fast. And don't shave, Renato!"

Goodness, she's flawless! What shiny hair! observed Heather. Veronica wore bright pink lipstick on the poutiest lips in Illinois. And she was kind. Heather wished she didn't hate her, but there was no need to deny it.

Veronica began, "I just got word. People are wondering where you and the girls are, and Sylvia claims you broke into the store and stole her money."

Heather had the money in her purse by her side as Veronica spoke. Heather found interest in how Veronica kept up with the trivial events of their little farming town, even knowing the names of nobodies. She stared at Veronica as she spoke. Golden blond curls framed her face, showing off distinct cheek bones that showed off her pink lipstick. Her baby-blue dress flowed in the breeze beautifully. Heather then noticed Renato; his chin rested long with his mouth slightly resting open. Veronica finished speaking and looked at Renato, startled for a split second, noticing how he stared. She stared back.

"Did you hear me, Renato?" She smiled at him through her words.

"So am I in trouble?" He sounded like a 10-year-old.

"Well," her face became a bit more serious, "the store was trashed a great deal. Windows broken, everything in the store a mess, Mr. Hugh's safe was empty."

Renato wrinkled his brows and deepened his concern with a backdrop of a smile. "The safe was already broken. Hugh never kept anything in there."

"Renato, where are you going?" Veronica asked with her hands out, "And why do you have the girls? Did their mother not want them?"

Did she not think I could answer? Did she think I was too little to think without her or Renato around? Heather simmered. She took a few steps back to eat her oatmeal. Heather needed distance from Veronica. Heather didn't plan on staying with Renato much longer. She had no plan, but she didn't expect Renato to be part of it. Still, Heather hoped he wasn't growing bitter towards her, feeling forced to be with her.

"Police involved?" Renato asked, ignoring her question regarding Momma.

"I think so, yes," Veronica answered.

Mae sat eating her oats, too distracted by the fire and people and horses to listen. Renato stared at Heather. She turned back to look at the distant land that rolled on for miles. There was peace over there.

"She's not a mother, and she didn't want the girls," Renato said. He stared at Veronica as he admitted, "I can't let her." Renato was playing the hero, Heather thought to show off in front of Veronica. Renato had earlier said they needed to talk. Heather wondered what about.

Within the minute Heather planned to ask Veronica for a ride back to Sterling, the plan squashed.

Veronica gazed at Renato as if satisfied with his answer. She removed keys from a tiny purse and dangled them above Renato's hand resting by his side. "Take my car."

"What?" Renato murmured, cupping the keys.

"To New York?" Mae asked, walking over from the fire. "Yes! We found a way!" Mae still dreamed. Heather pierced her eyes at Mae as if irritated.

"Here, take my car to the River North Resort," she demanded his attention. "You've been there." Renato took the keys. "My family owns a large portion of it," she looked around and added, "You can't stay here, and even if you haven't told me where you're going, I'm quite sure you're not going back to Sterling, now, are you?" Veronica lowered her voice and her head as if her head controlled her volume. "I'm well acquainted with the clubhouse's owner — a distant relative -- and I own a suite. You three can get properly cleaned up."

Renato must have felt the need to flirt. "You sure you want to hoard a criminal like me? What is that, aiding and abetting? I could get you into some big trouble." He smiled softly at her, hoping she wouldn't take this serious situation seriously at all.

Goodbyes were short, but Mae hugged Saint William as if she'd known him more than a day.

They fit into the front seat of Veronica's 1927 Stearns Knight automobile. The lap of luxury under a sunny winter sky, headed south. Mae sat between Renato and Heather in the front. They petted Mae more than usual; she had to sever her eternal connection with Saint William and was fragile at that moment. Not to mention they let her think they were traveling north.

"When I get home, I'm gonna grab Daddy's thick cardigan sweater and wrap up in it. I've been so cold all the time," Mae said with a soft sad voice. Her hopes and plans pierced Heather's chest.

"Wait," Heather said. "Ren, this is crazy. This is not right." Heather asked Renato to talk outside the car. Renato left the motor running and stepped out. They stood at the back of the car. Heather looked around to see no one staring.

"Maybe we should go home," Heather said. Renato shook his head in disappointment. "Well," she continued, "maybe just Mae and me. You can keep going. Go on home to Savannah. I release you."

"Let's go!" Mae shouted from inside the car.

"What? Alright," Renato said and threw up his hands. "I thought you wanted to go, too," Renato said, staring at Heather. He walked back to the driver's door.

"I do, Ren. But maybe this isn't the right way. You know," she voiced with less confidence, "I left the store a mess, the police might be involved, Momma's mad, and I'm lying to my sister."

'Heather, you wanna go home? Go home. You don't have to explain it to me."

"I won't keep you from going to Savannah. Then, everyone will be happy."

Renato turned around, placed his hands in his pockets, walked back to Heather, and leaned against the car.

"You'll be happy?" He gave in a deep breath, and at his exhale, he looked at Heather and answered, "Okay," he nodded his head slowly and then added, "What's wrong with you? You're so used to dreaming all the time, you don't want to see life happen. What are you shooting for, good enough? Are you scared?"

"Of course" —

"Let's go!" Mae shouted again.

"You're good with Sylvia gettin' her slimy hands on Mae? Hell no," Renato chuckled. Heather was stunned — Renato cared for Mae. "She's plotting against me, Heather." He stared into Heather's eyes to confirm belief. "You don't need me, I know. You've made that clear," he added.

A T-Model clattered up the road, grabbing Heather and Renato's attention. It looked familiar, and they recognized the silhouettes of the Hawks propped inside the car.

Heather and Renato climbed in Veronica's car and sandwiched Mae. They ducked and watched the Hawks pull up the long driveway. Renato rolled away from the barn discreetly. They found the main highway and headed south.

Heather held a small straw of hay she pulled out from a bale and took from the barn.

18

A Rich Ride

A bottle of scotch escaped from Renato's satchel and rang and banged and rolled in the back floorboard.

"That needs to go in the trunk," Renato said, and he pulled to the side of the long, straight road and stopped. He stepped out and grabbed the bottle as Mae and Heather sat in the car and waited for him.

"Uh, Heather?" Renato called as he stood with the trunk opened, "You may want to come see this." Mae and Heather quickly joined Renato over the opened trunk, and Heather found a treasure. There before her eyes was an array of shopping bags and boxes with hats, shoes, dresses, and more accessories than she ever had in her possession.

How does a lady forget about a trunk stuffed full of new dresses, new hats, new stockings? . . . What else? Shoes to match?

Veronica had said nothing about these new treasures. It all looked like several recipes to sexy. A beige day-dress with coral polka-dots lay on top in a clear plastic. Underneath lay a coral cloche. Heather dug for more treasures, feeling victoriously sneaky. She dug out a baby blue dress and a blue turban hat, a pair of tan Louis heels and a pair of black pumps. A green pant suit screamed rebellion as Heather shouted, "Yes!" A plastic cushioning lay on the bottom of the trunk; Heather stared. Something was underneath. She lifted the plastic to reveal a shimmer of thousands of sequins sewn onto a black tube of material by some smiling seamstress knowing the body that fit into this dress would behold new heights of womanhood. This dress was now Heather's. *Yes, they're all now in my possession.* She stood in the middle of Renato and Mae as Renato held open the trunk. Her excitement cracked through her fake composure as that shining ray of woman enveloped her eyes. She smiled big and giggled in girly victory. Veronica had left her new clothes in the trunk. Heather felt obliged to make good use of them, especially in Savannah.

They stopped a couple of times as they drove on, once to trespass into someone's outhouse, and another time to eat some wrapped snacks Renato had with him. They drove all day. Mae continuously asked if they were almost in New York. Heather thought they had to have been almost in Georgia.

"We're north of the Ohio River," Renato answered. Mae didn't know, but that meant they were still in Illinois.

"Renato, you ever wish someone was dead to make your life easier?" Mae repeated Heather's earlier question.

"You wish I was dead, Mae?" Renato asked.

"That's the same thing I said to Heather when she asked me. The same thing!"

Renato looked over at Heather. "Who does Heather want dead?"

"Nobody!" Heather quickly answered.

They drove on in silence. About a mile or more of the road was scattered with limbs, sticks, and leaves like casualties from the tornado, and Renato spoke up, "I've wished people dead before. An old teacher in Savannah. Mr. Allen. He said this. He said . . . my presence in the Negro schoolhouse was a wicked act. That's what he told me," Renato glanced over in confirmation at Mae and Heather. "He told me to go to the white school, and I told 'em, 'Mr. Allen, they don't want me there,' and he told me, 'We don't want you here either.' Pissed me off! I wished many times he'd die," Renato shook his head looking ahead at the road. "But I'd show up in the building, and there he'd be. Mr. Allen, there'd he be! He probably saw my disappointment. . . I sure as hell saw his." Heather and Mae didn't answer.

"What'd you do? Go back to the white school?" asked Mae.

"No, I just stayed at the dock, the port. Your Daddy'd get home from school and tell me what he learned. Then I'd tell him what I learned."

"What you learned? At the dock?" Mae asked.

"I learned. I learned a bunch of stuff. How to make a still, . . . how to drive a boat, ocean life, . . . good whiskey, bathwater gin," Renato glanced over at them with a grin. "I taught Hugh!" They continued down the road staring straight ahead. Heather thought of Hugh smiling, standing on a dock with a glass of whiskey. She figured Mae and Renato were thinking about Hugh, too.

"I think I wished my pa dead once or twice," Renato continued. Mae and Heather both turned their heads to look at him. "I know. That sounds bad, I know it does. But I was Puerto Rican, and with a stronger accent than I have now. I noticed like everybody else. And I- we were the rum-running family, you know. . . the Puerto Rican crowd that comes to make things worse. Maybe they had a point, I don't know." Heather loved hearing her father and Renato tell stories about Savannah.

". . and if Pa was dead, well, I thought I could make a new life for myself instead of wading in the marsh, wearing smelly waders every day. If Pa died, I thought I'd be a normal kid. I wanted to be a cook. A chef. Go to work in a kitchen."

"You hate your father," Mae testified.

"No, I love my father. I thought I hated him when I was younger and stupid, Mae. I don't think like that anymore."

I don't want to hate Momma, and I'm a grown woman, Heather silently revealed. Sylvia left Heather, made her feel like a nobody, but Heather didn't want her mother dead. Heather often wondered if Sylvia missed her daughters. She hoped her mother did.

"Ah!" Renato blurts out in a laugh, "and Betty Dran's mother!"

"Another?" Mae asked. "Hell, Renato! How many people you wanna kill?"

He smiled, ignored her question, and looked ahead as he drove.

"Betty was a pretty white girl that used to go down to the

Savannah River with me sometimes" — he paused, "well, her ma hated me! And one time she asked me, 'Renato, do you drink liquor?' and I answered, 'Yeah, you want some?' She told me I was going to jail *and* to hell," Renato laughed loudly and said, "Betty left me alone after that, and I wished her ma was dead."

"You don't take a liking to mothers, do you?" Heather bantered. He looked over and gave a slight smile.

"I guess I wish Veronica Nolan was dead," Mae offered. Of course.

"Why, Mae," Heather started with elated curiosity, "do you want that woman dead? You're in her car, you know!"

"Heather, I wish she was dead for you," Mae answered. Heather scoffed.

"Uh, no. I don't want her dead," Heather lied.

"Well, if she's not dead, you can't keep those clothes in the trunk," Mae said.

Just before dusk, they pulled into the River North Resort - a grand gem! The hotel rose six floors from the green, manicured ground. Statues of birds and angels stood on stone platforms surrounded by beautiful bushes and flowers. Decorative engravings around fountains lavished the front lawn. One of the fountains shot twenty feet of water straight up and fell into a dancing circle, spraying a mist of water on their car as they passed. A glistening stream sparkled under a bridge they rolled over, and this posh hotel was powerfully capable of masking woes, miseries, and secrets so nobody shouts them aloud. Heather didn't see a single trace of that Depression Sterling kept convincing everyone about.

19

A New Woman

The late afternoon purple sky glamoured the resort. The driveway to the resort was lined with perfectly trimmed bushes and trees, standing like faithful toy soldiers. In a few yards the driveway divided; the right path disappeared under a forest, but through and above the trees at a distance revealed the top of a pale-yellow mansion. To the left, where Renato drove, a large white hotel with six floors stood wide enough to not see the other end easily. Behind the hotel Heather caught a glimpse of tennis courts and a large lawn with a border of a forest at a distance. The stream wound through and met them a second time beside the drive, in front of the hotel, reflecting every color around it. Renato passed the main entry way in the front of the hotel.

"Where are you going?" Heather asked.

"There's a locked door on down that should take us straight to Veronica's suite. I've made deliveries here before," Renato parked the car outside a single closed white door shaded with a white awning and a brick walkway.

"You've made deliveries to Veronica's room?" Heather

asked. Mae laughed. Renato ignored the question.

Heather took all she could carry from the trunk to inside the hotel. They took an elevator up to the fifth floor which opened to a long hallway of royal blue carpet. Beautiful chandeliers hung overhead, spaced out down the hallway. Engravings trimmed the walls and the ceiling for the entirety of the hall, including each door. Upon opening Veronica's door, windows — large windows! They stretched from the floor to the ceiling on one entire side of the main room, and they could see a great distance of the tops of trees and green rolling hills. Heather felt like a queen! A queen with new clothes bundled in her arms and a view of the world. She stood and stared at the same view the tops of all the trees could see, open and free.

The one-bedroom suite centered a large bed in the bedroom. The bed sat high with tall bed posts in each corner holding a canopy of mauve silk. Heather plopped the packages onto the bed.

Yes, my bed, for now. I made it here. I earned it. It's mine.

"I suppose I'll take the couch," Renato said with a grin, and he sunk into the living room couch with Hugh's hat over his face. The evening was restful. A hotel attendant came to the room, providing more necessities than they ever had at home. A lady in a starchy apron and black dress drew Mae a hot bath. A gentleman in a starchy suit rolled in a tray full of food — potatoes, chicken, fruit, bread, and maple syrup.

"Just like New York City! Just like I dreamed it!" Mae exclaimed.

"We're not in New York!" Renato snapped. Renato spoke with a hotel attendant about making a phone call to

Savannah. The plan was to be picked up by Renato's brother Isaac in a day or two. Until then, they would stay at the hotel.

Heather ignored them and was pulled to open every package from Veronica's trunk. She tried on everything. She wore the long flowing polka dot dress with the matching straw hat with a brim so wide it could shade her shoulders. She pampered herself with Sylvia's face powder and lipstick that Heather snatched before they left home. The dress billowed in a dance around her with each step.

"Wow," Renato said, "You going somewhere?"

"This is my traveling outfit when Isaac gets here," Heather answered. "I'll pay Veronica back. From Dodge Grocers. These are mine now." Heather had no plan to give Veronica any money, but Hugh would tell her it was the dignified thing to do.

"You sound like a bootlegger," he smirked. He lit a cigarette, a well-earned smoke.

After he lit his cigarette, he asked, "Where you going, Sterling or Savannah?"

"I don't know," she answered.

"New York?"

"I don't know," Heather said, irritated. "What are you gonna do in Savannah? You gonna keep bootlegging?"

Bootlegging was a business, and Renato didn't flinch at Heather's insult. His business was illegal, but a money-maker. And although it was illegal, Renato often voiced his disagreement with the law concerning prohibition. Some bootleggers, — not Renato, but some — thought the rebelling part was fun while making money. Renato had mentioned this "stupid way of thinking" to Hugh in the store.

"That's why some of them are dead," Renato told Hugh.

"Then stay out of it," Hugh responded.

He ignored Hugh as he washed potatoes. "Heather, did I ever tell you about my potato truck?" he leaned in on the store counter and looked excited. "My last time in Savannah was in a potato truck. I left it parked in Chicago. Hugh and Mr. Whitney picked me up and brought me here. To something stable." Mrs. Whitney's nephew partnered with Renato, and Mrs. Whitney became their middleman.

"Stable, Ren? I find that word to mean the same as boring," Heather answered. Renato knew many of the roads connecting the north and south. Knowing routes and where they lead was stability even when moving.

Renato also knew the hotel; he supplied their scotch for several months. He had a bottle for them. Heather took off her hat and jewelry and walked back towards the bedroom. "So, you done breaking the law? Did you finally listen to Daddy?"

"Hugh was thankful for every glass I gave him, now, wasn't he?"

Heather walked into the bedroom, and thought of Savannah, where her dreams lived. She turned around back to the doorway and asked Renato, "Does Savannah have palm trees?"

"Tons of 'em. Everywhere, Heather," Renato said, still lounging on the couch. He wiped out her picture of palm trees, and she stared at him, baffled.

"With coconuts?" That was all she could come up with.

"What? . . . No," he answered, "none that I've seen, but

have you ever seen a live oak tree draped with Spanish moss?" Heather stared at him waiting for more, "The trees' trunks — they're massive, too big to comprehend, like the sky, or . . . Heaven. The branches are so thick you could make your bed on one, and they hold these gray curly trails of Spanish moss as if they've been holding on to something for a long time. Something they love. They look like they fell out of a photograph into real life."

Heather stared at him the whole time of his description.

"I did nothing more than describe a tree, Heather," he stared back. "You're truly a romantic." He got up from the couch and hollered for Mae to hurry out of the bathroom they all three shared.

Mae got out singing nonstop. The hotel provided Mae with a wardrobe, "compliments of Miss Nolan."

"And you wanted her dead," Heather joked.

"So did you," Mae looked up and cut her eyes at Heather.

Mae and Heather strolled around the resort for quite a while, leaving Renato in the room as he readied himself to meet old acquaintances in the resort's speakeasy.

Heather followed Mae. They passed a spacious, empty ballroom that showcased a grand chandelier as big as a car, hanging in the center of the room. They strolled through a courtyard of men and women socializing. She was intrigued with the experience, with the lifestyle, and particularly with the hired entertainment.

They met two Black women in a back hallway. Despite the obvious connection, Heather and Mae's faces implied they needed some direction, as the women were frequents at the hotel. More than that, they were performers in the hotel's speakeasy. "Hoofers" they called themselves. Mae was determined to share her life story with them. She kept a close distance between the ladies and herself as they walked down the hallway, chatting and soaking in every word they spoke as a melodious golden truth. She beamed of how their Momma was in New York City waiting for them, and if they ever heard of her.

"Your Momma sounds like quite the berries," they doted over Mae, and they showed them their green room set up back-stage. A line of shiny dresses hung on one wall, and a long vanity table with a wide mirror and lights lined another wall. They were invited to a fluffy couch. Heather and Mae were pampered.

"Why don't you talk? You keeping secrets?" one of the ladies asked and sat across from Heather, staring at her.

The two ladies offered to give Mae and Heather new hair dos, relieving Heather of answering the question. Mae followed Hilda to a chair. The other lady, Doris, stood behind Heather, brushed her hair, and quietly asked, "Your Momma really in New York City?"

"I don't think so," Heather answered. She kept brushing.

"You in trouble?" she asked.

"I don't know yet," Heather answered. She felt like a child.

"This Renato cat. Is he a caper or the bee's knees? You can tell me," she said. Heather wasn't sure what to say.

"He's a friend," Heather answered.

"Just a friend? You're as gorgeous as Sheba! And I know, well, I know who Renato is. He's a catch. And you two are staying in one hotel room? That's what you're telling me?"

Heather stared ahead a bit baffled.

She continued, "OK, then the bank's closed, can I ask just that?"

Heather was still baffled. *The bank? What?* She said nothing. In no time Doris placed tiny rollers in Heather's hair with an oil and was already sliding them out. She shaped Heather's hair into a new woman. Wavy curls were polished and designed around her face. Heather thought she looked out of her realm, and it took her a few minutes to adapt; but ultimately, she felt beautiful. Purposeful.

"Good, then keep that stupid look off your face like you have no control," Doris told Heather as she sat in front of her again. "What's happening? From one Negro to another, what are you doing?"

"I'm headed to Savannah, to live my dream," Heather confessed.

"Baby doll, if you can't live your dream here, you can't live it anywhere," she snapped softly. "It don't matter where you go, it's still you!"

"Alright . . ."

"If you gonna tiptoe 'round here, you'll do the same in Savannah!" Doris stared at Heather as if disappointed. Heather said nothing. "Girl! Are you listening to me? Speak up! Nobody's ever gonna *give* you permission to speak up! You better learn to do it on your own!"

"I'm going to Savannah to find the man of my dreams," Heather spilled out, "A black sweaty man." Doris asked for it, and she smiled.

"Yes, that's right!" her voice sang back to Heather, "a good black man sweats out stories. It's true!" She narrowed her eyes and asked, "But what does a Puerto Rican man sweat?"

Heather smiled at her jesting. Before Heather left, Doris placed a sequined pin in Heather's hair, and insisted she go to the speakeasy.

"Men will be falling at your feet. Stay firm, doll! Don't smile too easily!" Doris and Hilda lectured Heather. "Strong women don't smile too easily," they said.

Mae, who received the biggest, fluffiest hairdo they had ever seen, stayed with the ladies as Heather rushed to their suite with intention. She had the outer shell of a woman. Perhaps strong credentials to go to the speakeasy on her own. By herself. *Maybe Renato won't recognize me.* She pulled the plastic off the lovely sequined black dress from Veronica's stash and slipped it on. Its length reached to the floor. The dress constantly twinkled. Heather's neck and chest were bare, and the lining was a low-cut revealing that the dress pressed upward on her breast, giving them fullness. Heather felt rich but terrified to go out of the suite wearing the dress. She revealed more than she ever had in her life outside of the bathroom. She purposed to walk quickly. She knew where to go. She strapped the black shoes on her feet, took a deep breath, and looked for a cigarette. She just needed to calm her nerves before going. With a couple of puffs, Heather relaxed, checked her lipstick and makeup. . . She stood feeling great for a moment as she dabbed out the cigarette, and Heather quickly walked out the door with her head forced high.

Women acted relaxed. Whether they really were, Heather didn't know. But they could act it.

20

The Dance

*H*eather was 19. She encouraged herself to keep walking. She had no intention of staying in her room. She wasn't a child, and she needed more confirmation for herself. How that looked, she didn't know. Heather was only 19.

She ventured to find the speakeasy. A metal door, cornered beside a stairway, was labeled "Hotel Attendants Only." She saw some beautiful people open and walk through the door, overly dressed for anyone attending a hotel. Heather met eyes with an elevator attendant as she walked towards the door. He showed no curiosity in her actions, so she pulled open the door and walked through. Descending concrete steps was the only option ahead. Nothing glamorous; it looked like a passage for workers, not for a woman in a black sequin dress. At the bottom of the steps, Heather chose to turn right down a long, empty hallway. Fewer lights were shining, and the hallway gradually dimmed. She questioned her direction. Perhaps she should have turned left.

She continued and found two thick double doors muffling music inside. Heather opened one of the doors and entered the dark room, full of hats on men's heads, and tables and booths and dancing. Beautifully dressed women walked slowly, as if they were content in their lives having nowhere to go. A bartender, with countless bottles as a backdrop, prepared drinks. Heather gravitated towards him and sat down. Hilda and Doris were on stage. They were dressed in beautiful long sparkling dresses, and their hair was shiny and wavy, their faces beautiful.

Heather remembered their advice: "Don't smile too easily."

"A scotch please," she requested, determined not to smile. The bartender stared at her for a moment, and a voice redirected his attention.

"It's on me," Renato said. He was dressed in a dark suit and was clean-shaven. He took off his hat, revealing his clean combed-back hair. He was strikingly debonair. He sat beside Heather and struck a light on a match to offer her. She lit her cigarette, and no one can smile when they light a cigarette. Renato stared at her rather placidly, and Heather kept not smiling. She wasn't surprised at his stare. He had practice staring at women who looked good as if he didn't care. She was now in the same group of beautiful women. Not that this was a goal of hers. Heather didn't even know for certain Renato would be there in the speakeasy. She probably assumed, but she told herself she just wanted to be a woman in a crowd.

"Don't you think this is edging on being a bit dangerous?" Renato asked. "You can't go out looking this beautiful.

Everyone will notice and stare. I can't kill everybody in here."

"Didn't Veronica tell you not to shave?" Heather mentioned.

"Why, do I look bad?" Renato jested as he rubbed his jaw.

Heather said nothing. She figured he had his gun. *Would he really shoot someone?* she wondered. All the same, Heather had to concentrate on not smiling. He noticed.

"What's wrong, Heather? You look mad." Heather didn't want discord between them, so she deflated her false composure and relaxed her face.

"No, Ren," she answered. "The singers on stage told me I shouldn't smile."

"Oh . . . I like that," he turned to face the crowd, leaning his back against the bar beside Heather. "I guess the bad guys will walk away. Yeah," he stared into the crowd. "I probably would have walked away if I didn't already know you're a sweetheart." Smiles were exchanged. Heather surrendered. One of the singers began a new song.

"Hey, Heather, . . . let's dance. You wanna dance with me?"

Heather smiled for a second time, took his hand, and her heart fluttered. His hand hugged her own hand. She paused to gulp her scotch. They walked to the dance floor. Renato placed his arm around Heather's waist and the other hand held hers.

"You remember when Mrs. Whitney and Old Man Whitney taught you and Mae how to dance?" Renato asked, smiling, even with his eyes. Heather wished he hadn't brought up Sterling. Memories swelled like a sickness. He stared waiting for Heather to take part in the conversation, but she didn't want to talk about Sterling.

"Heather, what's wrong?" he asked. Heather realized then that she couldn't leave the pains of her past, her childhood, of her Daddy's death. Heather as a girl in Sterling was what Renato remembered, and it made sense. So many good, good memories. So much pain. Couldn't he see? She wanted to keep going forward and changing. Renato couldn't be blamed for how he always knew her. But maybe it pulled her back, like being patted on the head. Heather resorted back to not smiling.

Renato drew his head closer to the side of her own and tightened his arm around her.

He whispered in her ear, "Stop thinking, please, and just dance with me." Renato slid more of his arm around her and embraced her closer, against him. They brushed the sides of their faces together, and Heather felt the warmth from his cheek. She smelled the mix of scotch between them. He placed his cheek close to her temple; he needed to be held, too. Renato brought the hand he held to his chest. Doris sang as if a mix of the trumpet and bells was what her heart sounded like.

Heather and Renato swayed slowly side to side, adhering to no tempo, adhering to no tension, to no thoughts. She felt the smoothness of his shaved jaw. Renato's arms felt like home. He wasn't a stranger anymore, and for the first time in Heather's life, she wanted to stay where she was.

21

The Morning News

A pounding fist at the door woke Renato and Mae early the next morning.

"Renato? It's Veronica!" muffled the other side of the door. She carried on with an aggressive pound.

Heather was already awake, clean and dressed in Veronica's polka dot dress. When she heard Veronica's voice, she threw the dress off and slipped on her own dress. Heather stuffed Veronica's clothes in the boxes and bags they came in. Mae sauntered out of bed, and she and Heather joined Renato in the living room. He unlocked the door, and Veronica stomped in quickly with a newspaper in her hand. She walked so straight it looked as if a string was attached to the top of her head pulling her towards the ceiling. She sat on the couch, still and upright as ever, and carefully not turning her head. Renato stumbled to a basin of water to splash his face.

"I have this morning's newspaper. I imagine many have set eyes on it already," Veronica stated as she turned towards

Renato with her shoulders and glanced at Mae and Heather. Her voice shook. They stared at her curiously.

"Freshly squeezed orange juice, that'd be good," Renato mumbled.

Veronica held the newspaper in front of her face and read, "'Wanted: Public Enemy, Robber, suspected Murderer and Kidnapper Renato Reyes-Sanchez.'" She looked at Renato. They all looked at Renato. He nodded as he dried his face.

"I'll have juice sent up!" Veronica sternly glared at Renato and focused back on the newspaper in her face. "Kidnapped! The daughters of singer Sylvia Washer."

¡Coño!" Renato chimed in a growling whisper, "Interesting she didn't use her married name." He sat beside Veronica on the couch.

Veronica continued, *"Renato Reyes-Sanchez – a Puerto Rican, associated with the Chicago mafia, kidnapped two young girls: Mae, age 9, and Heather, age 14, daughters of the well-known singer Sylvia Washer. Mrs. Washer recently became a widow after her husband was murdered. The murder is still under investigation. Mrs. Washer is now left to mourn and suffer without her beloved daughters. Sylvia believes the girls may have been drugged or beaten, and/or threatened by the Puerto Rican outlaw. Furthermore, Mathias Huntington, late friend of Singer Washer, was found dead with gunshots. Reyes-Sanchez is a top suspect. He is barbaric and dangerous. Mrs. Washer has yet to receive a ransom letter. 'I hope and pray my children are still alive!' says Mrs. Washer. Renato Reyes-Sanchez is at large, and authorities request all citizens to be on the lookout and to keep their children close by. If anyone sees or has seen a Puerto Rican man with two Negro girls, immediately report their last seen location to authorities."*

"Why do authorities care? Why would anyone care? We're colored. Nobody's looking for us." Heather said.

"You're just the bait, Heather. . . . They want the mob," Renato answered, stood up and walked to the back of the sofa. He stayed quiet for a moment. "This is bad. I'm in trouble. No one likes things shaken up." Renato leaned his hands on the table and stared out the window. "Everybody's gonna' be after me. Sylvia cornered me. I knew it, too. This is bad."

"It's my fault!" Heather began, "This is because of me!" Everyone stared at nothing, dumbfounded and quiet for a few moments until Renato spoke.

"Sylvia didn't know the ages of her own daughters? Huh! No doubt she's still singing and spilling out her breasts on stage as she's *suffering!*"

Heather was 14 five years ago. No one knew her age. She wasn't kidnapped. Renato took care of them. Protected them. It didn't matter how old Heather was; she was still a child.

"You a mob man, Renato?" asked Mae.

"No, and don't ask stupid questions."

"Well, the newspaper says you are." Mae stood in the middle of the living room, visible to all, with her hands on her hips.

"It also says you're 9 years old," Renato retorted.

"It's close."

"No, it's not, and I'm no mobster. I got a couple a . . . business . . . colleagues in Chicago. Mob men, yeah, but nothing too crazy," Renato got quiet with a smile behind a placid face. He was reminiscing again. "We even went to a Cubs game together. You know, I'm not so stupid to get on their bad side, but now . . . I guess I am."

"Oh, hell! He's a mob man!" Mae exclaimed, gazing at Heather with a smirk, "He does carry a gun, you know!" The seriousness of all this had not hit Mae yet.

"Shut up, Mae," Renato said and plopped down beside her. "Mae, we're being hunted. You, too."

"Let's just find Momma and tell her the truth," offered the pragmatic Mae.

"Momma knows the truth, Mae," Heather explained and began to pace the room. "She told the police Ren might kill us! She knows Ren won't hurt us. She knows!" Heather was mostly convinced of this.

"Renato, what are you going to do?" Veronica asked. Heather noticed Veronica's voice chimed so pretty after hearing her own voice.

Renato leaned back and spoke quietly, "You mean to dodge a bullet? Or . . . when there's a knock at the door? Or how I'm leaving this hotel? I don't know. I don't know nothing yet."

"I'm going to see what I can do to get you three some help," Veronica said.

"Wait, what do you mean? Who are you going to talk to?" Renato asked.

"Don't worry. I have clout here," Veronica sounded irritated as she folded up the newspaper.

Heather informed Mae they needed to hurry and leave.

"I don't wanna go any more," Mae said. "I'm staying here. I can start a career here." She didn't bring up going north nor Sterling nor New York City.

"You can leave me. It's alright," Mae spit out. "Everybody that ever cared for me left me. Besides, I can find Momma by myself!"

"I'm not leaving you," Heather told her. Mae sat quiet, preparing her words in that cauldron she had stored in her head.

"I'm speaking of adults, Heather." There it was.

"I'm as adult as anybody."

"No, you're not," Mae commented.

"I most certainly am."

"Well, I don't wanna be! Adults leave their children and shoot daddies and join mobs. I don't wanna be an adult. Kids don't mess up like that. . . They don't! . . . No, they don't," She stomped off to the bathroom and slammed the door.

Veronica followed Mae and gently knocked on the door.

"Mae, let's dine together for breakfast," she said and then looked at me, "I'll bring you something to eat." Mae came out dressed quite nicely in a new dark blue dress. Veronica quietly closed the suite door behind them. That was the last time Heather ever saw Veronica.

"Ren, we're in trouble, aren't we?" Heather asked.

"Yeah." He packed and scurried to get ready himself, acting flippant. "Anyone who saw the paper will look for me. This resort has the paper. . . I don't know who's already talking, who's called the police."

"I'm sorry," Heather told him. She felt she forced Renato into this position. A front-line position. Heather was scared of her Momma so she pushed Renato to the front line.

The morning was rushed. They had to go. Heather closed the bedroom door to clean up, dress, and pack. She recreated her polka dotted attire. All in anger. She didn't know why she was angry, but she felt like smacking Renato in his debonair face. She didn't know why. He didn't do anything. This was all Heather's idea to take her and Mae with him. Renato knocked on the door.

"Heather, let's talk," he said. Heather opened the door.

"Sit down," Renato said and motioned her to the couch. She joined him and saw a close up of the terror in his wide-open eyes. "I don't know what I was thinking. I'm at the mercy of time." He breathed deep and stared at Heather before continuing. He sounded apologetic for no reason.

"I'm sorry, Ren."

"Okay — no, I'm sorry," he said. "We gotta hurry before Mae gets back. The truth is I hate your Ma, Heather. I'm sorry to say that. You're nothing like her. I didn't kill nobody! And that bow-tie guy, thinking you were a money-maker," he said, leaning back on the couch, as if they had time for casual conversation, as if they had leisure time. Heather peered out the window. She wanted to leave.

He continued, "Hugh would never let that woman take you or Mae back with her. For your Daddy, whether you blackmailed me or not. So, it's not your fault, sweetheart."

He called her sweetheart. A second time. He was scared. Tears streamed down Heather's cheeks.

"Here's something else, Heather, . . .Sylvia! She's crazy," he continued, "Relentless! She wants that store, you know, but she needs the deed. I think she's heading South to find the deed to the store, that's what I'm thinking. She won't say that, you know. What she says is she's looking for you two. Like all this has nothing to do with money."

"Maybe there's a sliver of a chance that she is," Heather said. "Maybe she is looking for us." Maybe she was.

"Are you serious?" Renato stared at her. "Heather, no! Will

you stop letting her hurt you?"

"She's my mother, Ren, and I . . ." Renato sat quietly to give her a chance before he spoke.

"Mr. Haverson in Savannah — he's this rich guy, you probably heard Hugh talk about him — he may have the deed. If we can get down there before Sylvia, we can keep it out of her hands."

Mrs. Whitney had it, and Heather didn't say a word about it.

"What now? What do you want me to do?" Heather asked. She was ready to be just as relentless as her mother. Heather wished Doris could see her.

"Whatever you want to do. You can take Mae back with you to Sterling or take her up to New York so she'll shut up." They both smiled.

"I tell you what, you're free. You can ask someone at the front desk to take you back to Sterling. Police will be here soon. You choose, Heather." He gave Heather a great satisfaction she didn't realize she had longed for, a chance to choose.

But instead of feeling powerful, incompetence sank in. Renato gave Heather two logical choices. Mae and Heather could go back to Sterling and live life like they knew it. Heather could run the store. She'd be good. Secure. Stable. Or she could give Mae her dream and go to New York. Either way was a good, solid plan. Renato would be freed from kidnapping charges, and Mae would be happy.

Or Heather could live her dream and, somehow, save them all. She could try, anyway. But she struggled in thinking; what if she failed, all because of what she alone wanted? *And then what, live my dream and go on to Savannah? Was I thinking like Momma?*

"What do you want me to do?" Heather asked again.

Nobody's ever gonna give you permission to speak! Heather remembered Doris' words.

"Let's keep going," Heather said. "Let's go to Savannah. Mae might mess it up, and you might get caught, but I don't think- I don't think I want to let others decide what we want in life. Especially Momma." Heather knew Renato wanted to beat Momma at this. There were things they wanted in life, and Heather was tired of staring at them.

"It's dangerous, Heather," he remarked.

They were prey on that day forward. Heather's own mother was the predator. The wild beast. The newspaper article told the country Renato was dangerous. He was a target surrounded by thousands of gunmen. Yet, Heather was foolishly calm, lulled by the target.

A knock at the suite door reminded them of their danger. Renato opened it to two men dressed in suits.

22

Canis & Lee

"Canis and Lee," Renato said as the men ambled in the suite. Their eyes shifted quickly back and forth from Renato to Heather. Renato stepped backward.

"Run," Renato said casually. Heather couldn't comprehend his command. A pulse flooded Heather's head, and she didn't know if she tried not to move, or if she couldn't.

Hubert Canis and James Lee — Renato had said their names before in conversations with Hugh.

"Bad guys," Hugh told a younger Heather.

They were known as highway pirates, or "go-through guys," people said. They'd ambush and steal from the bootleggers. Canis and Lee were old war soldiers who experienced a darkness in oversea battles, lots of blood, like soldiers do. However, Canis and Lee perceived it differently.

Not sad or tragic. They wanted – needed — more blood. Back home in the States, a desire brewed in them to get their fix; it nagged them, like the need for a cigarette.

Hubert Canis's height towered over Heather, and his whitening hair on top of his long face with sparse red eyebrows gave him a ghostly look with flames above his eyes. His skin was so pale it looked almost translucent, like he already died. James Lee's perfectly round bald head was too big and looked so strong conveying how he, on the other hand, could never die, a discouraging look to enemies. The man had a forgetful face, but a memorable head size made up for it. Canis bent swiftly over Heather and pressed his massive hand over the lower part of her face, covering her mouth.

"Don't scream," Lee calmly instructed. He then plunged into Renato, snapping his fist against Renato's face. Renato's head flicked back with the punch, and his face was soon bloody. *He's going to die!* Heather was back in Dodge Grocers, and everything again went black.

Heather awoke. She lay on the couch. The day was predominantly bright, and sunlight brightened the living room of the suite. The sun carried promises on the day Hugh was murdered, too. Heather's ability to think rushed back. *The newspaper.* Heather's eyes rested on the ray beaming from the top of the window.

Where was Mae? The surroundings were too quiet if Mae was present. Forcing Mae to be helpless was vulgarity to the order of the world.

Heather lifted her head and saw Renato slumped in a chair with his hands lying lifeless in his lap. His lip and one side of his face were bright red and turning dark. A voice was dimly speaking despite the violent atmosphere.

"Reyes? Reyes-Sanchez?" the monotone, low voice rang in the room. Someone else, but all Heather could see was Canis towering over her.

Another man walked into her sight. A Native American wore a lime green suit with black patent shoes as shiny as his black hair, and he stood staring at Renato with his mouth rested open. He pulled a chair across from Renato and sat, securing his hair behind his ears. The confident demeanor, the lime suit, and no accent mismatched with his skin but showcased him remarkably.

"Reyes," he started again and introduced himself as Jacob Nettles. He motioned for the other two men to stand at the door. They instinctively obeyed him and stood post with the door behind them.

"They weren't supposed to hit you unless you tried to run. I'm, . . . ah!" he let out a low gasp. "I'm embarrassed! Are you thirsty?" He stood up looking around in disarray and then tiptoed quickly in his shiny shoes to a side table and picked up a bell, Veronica's bell. He then stopped and wantonly posed as he shook the bell. A man in the hotel uniform came in the door without looking at anyone but the man in lime. With a nod and narrow eyes, Jacob relayed orders quietly. The attendant turned around and left on his mission like he did this all the time. Heather watched Jacob fondly. He moved to a beat she couldn't hear.

"Where are the girls?" Renato asked. He didn't see Heather behind him on the couch.

"Well, Reyes, that's the whole reason we're here," aired out the man's voice.

"Where are the girls?"

Jacob stared at Renato for a moment before answering in a didactic, formal tone, "Behind you, like a faithful servant. The youngest is feasting. I've yet to meet her. Mae, I presume."

The attendant brought Renato a glass of spirits. Renato swallowed the drink quickly. The man rang the bell again as the attendant was walking out. The attendant paused and turned around. He forgot to leave the scotch bottle still in his hand. He quickly set the bottle on the nearest table and scurried out. Jacob turned back to Renato.

"Veronica requested of me to tell you goodbye for her. And then, she just left. She had to get going."

Renato turned his head to see Heather; he smiled with a corner of his lips.

"The beating shouldn't have happened," Jacob continued. "But it's truly your lucky day. They – those two men who visited you – they kill. All the time."

"I know Canis and Lee," answered Renato.

"Really? Yes, they're well-known. But this whole thing, it was a test. A test to see if the girls were a decoy for your sales." Jacob stood and faced Renato and Heather.

"You think I'm loading liquor?"

"Yes, Reyes," he answered. "That's what you do, and you haven't stopped by here in a couple of years to make a delivery. And now you show up . . . with nothing? What? Are you now in the business of selling Negroes?"

"I'm not in the selling business at all," Renato replied. "The girls are mine, more or less."

"They're not yours. They belong to some colored singing

woman named Sylvia." Jacob paused and stared at Renato, waiting for a reaction, smiling, "It all sounds curious, you can't blame me."

The man poured two more drinks. Heather wanted a drink, too. She wished she could speak up.

"Listen, Reyes, I'm not going to hurt you, but you're in my hotel. It's part mine, so mine." He smiled and looked at Heather staring at him. "You know, . . . I saw her, Miss Sylvia. I watched her perform last night in Pittsburgh. She dedicated a song to her kidnapped children. 'This one's for you, girls' she said, and she sang her heart out- this terrible song, I must admit. I don't mean to speak negatively of your mother." He looked back at Renato and asked, "You know her? Sylvia?"

"What's it to you?"

"I follow the law, Reyes. I appreciate the scotch you brought last night. Due time, though. Despite your poor business tactics and relations, and that I should turn you in, or kill you, or kill the girls, or take the girls for ransom, or slaves," his eyes switched from Renato to Heather, and he continued smiling with his drink in hand, "which I entertained the technical details of all these options . . . but I want to work with you, Reyes."

Heather stood not knowing which way she should go; but before a step was taken, Jacob hardly raised the low volume of his voice and said, "Please sit back down."

Heather slowly sat and said, "Renato needs the blood washed off his face. And I need a drink."

Jacob obliged, and he helped Renato over to the basin to wash his face, offering to help Renato clean his face. Renato repeatedly jerked away from Jacob's doting gestures. So awkward, Heather finally looked away. A wide ray of light shined on the right side of her face; she looked over at the wall of windows.

"Did they hurt you?" Renato asked in anger, appearing over her surprisingly. Heather stared at him. He had dried blood on his face and neck and splats and drops on his white collared shirt. He didn't wash his face completely. His lip was swollen as well as his left eye. Heather shook her head no. Renato patted his sides as if looking for something.

"Renato, why do you care if we touched her?" Nettles stood over Renato and studied them. "Is that not your business? Your product for sale?" Jacob asked. He strolled behind Renato and motioned for him to have a seat on the couch beside Heather.

"What are you talking about?" asked Renato.

"I'm willing to do business," Jacob pulled a chair closely in front of Heather and had a seat. "And the oldest is absolutely exquisite," he stared at her like she was a prize-winning mare. "Slave in every way, I presume?" He stood up, picked up the back of his chair, and motioned for Renato to follow him back to the chair behind Heather as if inviting Renato to his imaginary office. Renato sat again and said nothing. Heather waited for Renato to say something, something. Jacob noticed Heather's anxiety and observed her face.

Finally, Renato said, "We need to work out a different deal. We gotta get out of here unseen."

As Jacob sighed, Heather asked permission to go to the bathroom, and she stumbled away.

Heather washed her face as a deal was being made over her existence. She wished her Daddy was there. She missed him.

He would have a fit hearing a man go on about her being exquisite. Renato didn't. Heather concluded no one's having a fit over her like Hugh would, and no one else would again. She didn't have anyone to admire her clean face, but she scrubbed it clean anyway. Alone, she returned to the living room.

Jacob Nettles had a power of deviance. It was scary. His thoughts were evidently on an insidious trail.

Jacob monotoned his words, "We're coming close to our goodbyes one way or the other." With a smile he continued, "Reyes, wouldn't life be grand to be free to go anywhere?"

"I won't be free. Just jail for me. Or shot," Renato answered.

"I suppose if you like life that way," Jacob offered a facetious answer. "I'm fasting. You ever fast? Reyes?" He sounded like a friend sharing a secret, still with the deep voice of an Native-American white man. "I'm fasting and denying myself pain and suffering. Pain and suffering. I'm letting it go. It's not easy. It comes with a sacrifice." He lounged back in his chair facing Renato. "Denying my hand to dip in anything . . . solemn, anything dreadful. It takes intense focus. I must avoid the choices that make dreadful ripple effects. There's planning and preparation." His didactic philanthropy pulled Heather's attention.

"Sounds nice," she whispered as she stood still on the other side of the room. Nettles turned towards her and stared for a moment. Then he turned back with an inquisitive eye towards Renato.

"Hmmm, . . . does she . . . have your heart, Reyes?"

"Are we doing business or not?" Renato chimed in, keeping his voice on the same smooth plateau. Jacob stared at

Renato like a disappointed teacher. Heather slowly returned to the couch and sat. Jacob's eyes followed her.

"Reyes, I'll tell you — it looks like a complex situation. I want us to still be friends, or acquaintances. Business partners," Jacob nodded his head, agreeing with himself. "I once worked as a psychosis-therapy apprentice at an asylum in Virginia. So many experiments and so much research. These humans with — not less of a mind, and not more, but more colorful and less colorful. I saw so much." The softness of his voice lulled Heather into forgetting impending danger.

"I came to a conclusion. We all have an authority, and it's the world around each of us, you see. There are good people, and they should be rewarded, just like I believe the bad should be, and always are, punished. You two are not excluded." Jacob unwarily gazed at Renato.

"Reyes, you're a slave trader, a bootlegger of illegal live human goods," Jacob shared as if revealing new information. He sat back and stared at Renato with eyebrows raised in lecture form. Heather could speak for herself, but she was curious to see how this would play out without her interference.

"You give me the girls, and as a payment, you're off the hook. Free. Go on to your sunny Savannah, Georgia. Free," Jacob offered as he studied Renato's eyes and then continued, "One more thing, I'm not keeping the girls, just an experiment. Then they can go, too." Jacob reached in his pocket and pulled out a folded letter and a key. "You might still get shot or go to jail. I don't know how bad you've been. But it won't be by my guys." He reached over and gave the key to Heather and the letter to Renato.

"What is this?" Renato studied the paper, "A train ticket? A bus ticket?"

"It's the same thing here. One massive station. You choose which one you want to get on."

"Excuse me, Mr. Nettles," Heather interrupted, "He can't give us to you. He doesn't own us. Nobody does."

"Somebody has to. They must."

Heather's key was to unlock the door across the hall, where Mae was supposedly feasting. Jacob smiled at Heather, proud of himself. He explained that Heather's mother was invited to perform on that night and was expected to arrive shortly.

"Not only your mother, but police authorities should pour in the hotel any minute. Any minute! I'm sure one or two or three of my employees have already contacted authorities. They may have their own guns cocked, ready to be heroes," his voice smoothed out.

"Young girl," Jacob called Heather, "I'm not a demon; I'm a savior, and I will free you, but you've got to work for it." He leaned forward towards her in his chair. "Two extra bus tickets lie just under the tablecloth where your mother will sit," he glanced over to Renato with a smile, then back to Heather, "You'll have choices - your mother or two tickets to get the hell out of here, straight into the arms of your Puerto Rican bootlegger!" Jacob snickered with smiling eyes at Heather. "I don't know what you're going to choose! I can't wait to see!"

"I'll get them," Heather offered adamantly.

'You'll get what? You'll get the tickets? Why? You can reunite with your mother!" Jacob held out his hands in sarcastic confusion as he spoke. "She sang a song for you, didn't I tell you?"

Before Heather walked out of the suite, she shared a warm gaze with Renato.

"Don't worry. I'll steal you again," he softly claimed behind his puffy lip as he rolled up his sleeves.

23

Predator and Prey

Every step to the suite across the hall felt unpredictable. Vulnerable. Heather was surprised to see a lavishly adorned room with Mae doting around a table filled with food. Heather expected more destruction. Mae knew nothing of what had happened to Renato or her.

"What's wrong? What happened?" Mae asked Heather, staring at her with wrinkled brows. Heather told her to finish her meal quickly. Heather had no appetite, but she picked up a sweet roll and stuffed it in her mouth. Mae needed to eat as much as possible; Heather didn't know when or where their next meal would be. Mae selected two more bites, sensing the urgency, and they entered back into Veronica's suite. No one was there. Renato was gone. Not a trace of him was left.

"Where's Renato? Did he leave us?" Mae asked. Heather had to think about that later. They cleaned up, dressed, and packed all their new clothes. In between it all, Heather fought back tears. She didn't know where Renato was. She found her Dodge Grocers money still hidden in her purse. Not touched. It was like her secret super-power, she told herself, trying to console her grief. She thought she should have given some money to Renato. And she wondered again and again, where did he go?

Heather grabbed Veronica's bell and thrust it into her suitcase. Mae and Heather left their bags of new clothes and toiletries by the door in the suite and hurried through the downstairs halls to the lobby.

"Please, Mae, stay quiet."

A police officer was standing at the front desk. Mae and Heather stepped back unseen. Heather heard the desk attendant state, "Fifth floor." The officer then looked out the front doors and windows. Heather's eyes followed to see more police officers outside the door. Mae and Heather turned around and scurried down the first-floor hallway and out a back door around to the hallway where they first met Doris and Hilda. They found their dressing room, but they were nowhere to be seen. Heather sat for a moment, exhausted.

"Are we running from the police again?" Mae asked.

"Yes," Heather answered in between huffs.

"But we didn't do anything wrong. Why are we running?"

"Because, Mae," Heather didn't mean to sound aggravated, but she was overwhelmed, "I have to find Renato."

"But we can show them that we're fine. We haven't been kidnapped." Mae had a point, but Heather typically disagreed with her. She was younger, so she naturally had to be wrong.

"I can't let them stop me from finding Ren," Heather failed at explaining, and she fought tears again.

It was time to meet Momma. Heather didn't want to. Curled up in her bed, back in Sterling, just dreaming about Savannah felt like a happier place at this moment.

They stepped into the dark, quiet speakeasy from the side stage door. The atmosphere felt different than how it felt last night. A boring lull, a room recovering from being violated the night before. Heather felt young and uninvited. Mae walked beside her. Heather looked at Mae, and she looked different, not as confident. Heather felt sorry for her.

Sitting alone, legs covered by the overlap of the white satin tablecloth in a dark corner booth was Sylvia. Mae saw her and greeted her, "Momma!" Sylvia stared petrified at Mae and Heather as they walked towards her. No smile. Not a word for a moment. Mae and Heather slipped into the dark booth, Mae close beside Sylvia and Heather across from them. Mae wrapped around Sylvia, pulling Sylvia's body in as close as she had strength for. Heather suspected her mother must not have been told about this plan.

"Momma, aren't you gonna say something?" Heather demanded and taunted. "Haven't you been searching for us?" Heather's voice shook.

Sylvia looked irritated. "Heather, please don't tell me what I should and shouldn't say and do!" She blinked repeatedly, shifting her large eyes. Mae sat beside her mother on the booth and tried again to wrap her fat arms around her mother. Sylvia held onto the glass on the table as if she was holding someone's hand.

"Your search is over. You found us," Heather stated stoically with her voice still trembling.

"Where's Renato?" Sylvia asked.

"What does that matter?"

"I want to know where your kidnapper is, Heather! Don't sass me!"

"Momma," Mae interrupted. "Let's go to New York now! Us three! We're ready! We're ready!" Mae's glee built a suppressing feeling in Heather.

Sylvia looked in the distance with large eyes. Heather and Mae had her cornered, imprisoned. It gave Heather some relief. Heather settled across from them both. She traced her fingers along the tablecloth and looked for an outline of the paper tickets. There was nothing. If Heather knew Momma, she knew Sylvia wanted to do the wrong thing so bad and abandon them, but she was stuck. Sylvia stuttered and said words of no purpose. The officers wouldn't advance their search here. They weren't to know about this illegal hiding spot.

"Momma, we're headed that way. To New York," Heather lied. "You'll meet us along the way?" Heather was ready to part from her and satisfy Mae at the same time. Where were those tickets? Sylvia either played along with Heather for Mae's sake, or she thought Heather was stupid enough to believe she'd want to leave with them.

"Yes, go get packed up. We'll meet along the way."

"We're packed and ready," Heather answered. She saw Doris walk behind the bar pouring a glass of water. "Mae, you should tell Hilda and Doris, tell them goodbye. Quickly, Mae! Go! I'll come say bye soon."

Mae explained to Sylvia who Hilda and Doris were. Heather looked under the tablecloth quickly during their interaction.

Heather hunched over a bit to hide that half her arm was under the tablecloth. Sylvia held onto her drink on the table, propped beside her cigarette case, the one Heather once stole and got a beaten for. Mae walked away to Doris, and Heather receded her arm for a moment, snatched up the case, and lit herself a cigarette.

After a long breath of smoke, Heather exhaled her thoughts aloud to Sylvia, "Why are you not wanting us to go with you, Momma? Why are you not running to tell the police that the kidnapping is over?"

"Stupid girl!" Sylvia kept her head and body still and stiff as she spoke, shaking her head. Heather hated her mother's voice; a lump of all the toxins Sylvia stuffed into Heather's body was slowly coming up into her throat. Sylvia continued with the familiar cacophonous voice, "I am performing today. Soon. You probably know that, don't you! You have no right to tell me when I should do what. No right!" Her nostrils twitched and flared. She reached to cup her glass without lifting it. "You are my children! I'll take you when I'm good and ready. My children!"

"I'm not a child, Momma."

She ignored Heather. "If Renato's even still alive -but Heather, no! It's not time yet! Get out of here!" She spoke through her gritting teeth.

"What do you mean —if Renato is alive?"

They stared at one another as Heather stood to leave. Heather waited on an answer, and a smirk grew on Sylvia's face. "I am coming after you and Mae, but I'm not, I am not playing games with that Puerto Rican. He should be terrified every step he takes."

She wanted to find Mae and Heather on her own with no help -- they were her prey. She didn't want her daughters to drop into her mouth. She wanted to gnarl and snatch them when they had no hope. This was a game; Heather now identified as a playing piece.

She lifted the tablecloth as high as she could to see the tickets, hearing Sylvia's protests. Right before Heather snatched them, Sylvia pressed her hands on the tablecloth.

"What are you doing!"

Heather reached toward her and took her cigarette case. Heather made no secret about it. As Sylvia's attention rested on Heather's audacity to steal in front of her, Heather's fingers knew the direction under the tablecloth to slip the tickets off the table. She spun around and paraded out of the bar without looking back. Momma didn't call for her either.

"We're gonna miss the train! We better hurry," Heather tried to sound encouraging to Mae. Mae accompanied Doris and Hilda on the fluffy sofa in their dressing room. She eyed Heather with no urgency. Doris agreed to snatch their luggage from Veronica's suite and drive them to the train station.

"Can I say bye to Momma?" Mae asked.

"She won't be there, Mae," Heather answered. Heather didn't know where or what Sylvia would be doing, but Heather had a horrible feeling that Sylvia was plotting something dreadful. Heather wanted to get out of the River North Resort Hotel. And she wondered, *where was Ren?*

24

Many Colors

I t was a 1929 Willys-Knight automobile that got them to the train station. Mae and Heather shuffled into the car.

"A 66B Plaidside Phaeton, or something of that fancy sort," Doris explained, "It's not mine." She had picked the girls up at a back door and drove slowly around the side of the hotel. "Get down!" Police officers were walking around everywhere. Heather quickly folded over; Mae resisted.

"Mae, please!" Heather whispered.

"Girl!" Doris exclaimed. "You're not getting me in trouble. Get down!" Mae finally crouched down.

The car continued. Doris said, "Oh no. He's got his eye on me." The car kept rolling. "I just . . . smile and wave . . . And look ahead." A "Ma'am" and a "Stop" were shouted outside, but the car continued.

"Stay down!" Doris ordered. The car jolt into speed. "Okay, you can come up now. My Lord! That was crazy!" Doris roared out a laugh. They were on a main road, and Doris was zooming. Trees were a blur. She wisped off into farmland, a bumpy ride on rolling hills, and back onto a main road. Just before the train station came into sight, the sky grew white and then dark, and they were soon enveloped in torrents.

"If I wasn't going with Momma, I'd stay with you," Mae told Doris.

"Mae," Doris started, "You stay with your sister. And mind her!"

"I never learn anything minding all the time."

Mae and Heather parted from Doris into the rain. Doris helped the girls grab their luggage. Her hair limped around her smiling face, and she was more beautiful than any dream or wish either sister ever had.

Heather and Mae were directed to the front cart closest to the engine, the "Crow's Cart" as the ticket attendant called it. Officers were there, but they didn't seem to be on the lookout. The "Crow's Cart" was the Negro cart. They boarded in time.

"Where's Momma?" Mae asked.

"Where's she ever been, Mae?"

A cart full of colored folks. And on the back corner bench was Renato.

Heather grabbed Mae's arm to keep her walking all the way to Renato. He was there, waiting for them. He still had a slight scratch on his lip and a little discoloration under his eye. He smiled with his eyes and mouth, looking grateful and relieved and beautiful. Heather scooted beside Renato, and Mae beside Heather.

"Hi, Renato," Mae greeted him sadly but with sweetness.

"Hi, Mae," he answered. "Hi, Heather," he smiled at Heather. "They almost didn't let me on this cart because I'm not Negro," he laughed, staring at Heather calmly, inviting her to partake in the amusement.

Heather didn't know how she felt such a pull with no thought into it at all, but she leaned over, took the sides of his face in her hands, and kissed him on his lips. Her face then swelled with embarrassment.

"Let me sit by Renato," Mae insisted. She stood to squeeze between them. They looked tangled. Finally, Renato propped himself between them. Mae looked up at him as if her face was prepared for a landing of his lips. He kissed her on the forehead.

"Now quit acting stupid," he told her. He turned to look at Heather, and for no reason, they both responded to the eye contact with a startle. Heather looked down and out the window, not really knowing where to look. She didn't turn to see, but she thought Renato was doing the same. He didn't say anything.

Darkness comes in all sorts of shades in skin color and character. In his Puerto Rican skin, Renato never looked so white. He looked out of place. As the train found its momentum, it roared louder than the pouring rain and the thunder surrounding them. They gazed out the window through the dense specks of foggy rain. The station was long, a long way to be free from. At the end corner stood Sylvia and her plump bow-tie friend. Renato, Heather, and Mae stared at them in shock and caught Sylvia's attention.

"Momma!" Mae shouted. Heather's shock was more in what her mother was wearing; Heather gasped in terror — Sylvia wore a scarf smeared with a bright red flower print with a bright blue center, the same painted flower in the murderer's car when Hugh was shot dead. The same scarf that lay over the murderer's seat. Heather knew it was the same. Her heart fluttered and she felt nauseated.

Sylvia exchanged a mutual shock with a gasp and screamed, "Stop the train!" The train didn't stop, and momentum increased.

"Momma," Mae said softly, and she silently began to whimper. She was heartbroken. Heather tried to compose her own panting. Renato placed his arm around her, drawing Mae closer to him. Mae resisted. Heather didn't care about Mae's grief; their horrific expressions were for two different reasons.

"I'm sorry, Daddy," Heather whispered. Breathing is a conscious chore when in exasperated shock.

"You alright?" Renato asked. Heather nodded but told him they needed to talk. Heather could visualize the scarf lying over the back seat of the murderer's car. She felt the same fear sitting in the train that she had in the store just a few days ago.

"She came for us, Heather. She did!" Mae forced out in anger.

Why did she come? Heather thought for a moment that Sylvia may have had a change of heart after Heather left her at the speakeasy. Perhaps she came to the station to mend things. To make her wrongs right. Heather's mind was loaded with too many thoughts of someone that kept hurting her. She remembered feeling heartbroken just like Mae around her age. Momma gone again.

Sylvia told 12-year-old Heather, "I must go, Heather. To make money. It's a sacrifice, but it's so that we can have money." She abandoned Heather, but Heather thought her

Momma was so brave to plow the crazy world so she could provide for her two girls. She'd be gone for months. They wouldn't hear a word from her. The next time she came back to Sterling, she came in the store, and a cocky and younger Renato used to talk a whole lot more.

He told her, "Hey, Sylvia! What the hell do you want? You must need more of Hugh's money. Hugh!" He hollered toward the back of the store, "Sylvia's back for more money!" Sylvia slapped Renato with a great might across his face. Stunned him quite a bit and bloodied his lip, but it didn't stop him.

"¡Sea la madre!" Renato said quietly. Hugh had told him to keep his bad words in another language. "Sylvia, Heather's got questions for a mother. Should she be a lady, or bend over like you?" His words were harsh, but comforted Heather to think her own similar thoughts were okay.

"Shut the hell up, Renato! Where's Hugh?" Sylvia didn't turn to look at Heather also in the store with her.

"Oh! and Sylvia," Renato wouldn't stop, "while you're here, teach Mae how to read!"

"Hugh!" Sylvia hollered, "Why don't you go find a mafia bullet to put in your head!" Heather was old enough to know the mafia were scary people. *Chicos malos*, or "bad guys," Renato taught Heather.

Sylvia met with Hugh in the back office. Heather hurried home; she scrubbed and polished and cleaned every few steps in the house. She steamed a dinner of fresh vegetables, and she waited, and she waited for Sylvia to be their guest. She never showed up. Just Hugh. Sylvia told Hugh to let Heather and Mae know she had to get back to work. Heather felt as if she had failed. She didn't know how, but just that she had. Heather failed at switching off her heart for her mother. Heather had Mae go ask the Whitney's if they wanted to eat with them. They didn't, so it was the three of them with a fourth chair empty.

Now on the train, the thought of Sylvia coming for her children still tempted Heather to scrub, clean, and steam some vegetables for her Momma. But this time, the earnest of it dulled. The scarf pushed aside the mother-daughter dreams.

Heather regained a sense of calm for a few moments in the train, knowing they were free and headed South finally. It was the calm before the terrible Sylvia-storm. Renato paid attention to Heather and stayed silent, while Mae sat heartbroken. Heather reached over and grabbed her hand.

Silence and lack of motion derived from either peace, exhaustion, or despair.

"I knew those two men. The men in the room," Renato started a conversation.

"I know," Heather answered, but she was grateful for a topic that had nothing to do with Sylvia. "I knew them when I was a boy in Savannah. About Mae's age." Mae rested her head on Renato's arm and fell asleep.

"Chicos malos," Heather said.

"Yeah, chicos malos!" Renato continued, "I remember I walked up through the marsh into the woods, close to my uncle's car. He packed his car with liquor to go make some sales. I was gonna walk home and not bother him for a ride." Renato looked out the window as he reminisced, occasionally glancing at Heather with a smiling mask over his eyes.

"Uncle Renny —we had the same name —he was a big guy for a Puerto Rican, with a bald and really big head. He looked mean in his suit. Anyway, he stood by the front of the car when, out of nowhere, another car came driving up. Two men jumped out so quickly, Canis and Lee, one with a shotgun. He straightened out his arm and pointed the gun at Uncle Renny's face and shot. Renny fell back." Renato's voice softened to a whisper. He leaned his head back a bit. "The men took the boxes of liquor out of Renny's car and packed their own car. I crouched down and hid in the brush. I saw Renny crawl on his belly to the front of the car. All I could see was the top of his head, his broad shoulders, and his big hands carefully pressing down on the ground as if he was wholly depending on them to rescue him. His face was so bloody, and his face inches to the ground. Was he crawling toward me? My uncle was dying. These two killers were stealing from him, and I froze. I was too scared to go help my uncle," Renato bowed his head, rubbing his jaw. "I hid and watched the top of his head, his face close to the ground. His fat fingers trying to lead."

"Renato, I'm really sorry. I know you miss him. Like I do Daddy," Heather offered.

"Actually," Renato answered, "He survived the gunshot. He had a large scar and a shattered jaw. And I remember how big his eyes were, filled with fear when he was released from the hospital. I wondered if he'd be mad at me if he knew I just stared at him as he suffered."

"You were just a boy. Scared," Heather answered.

"Heather, I still am," Renato continued. "Canis and Lee couldn't have recognized me. They never saw me when they shot Renny."

Renato and Heather rested their eyes out the window at the dusk, flashing by quickly. Tall, skinny pine trees densely lined the train's pathway. Heather's excitement was pulled down with fear. *Who's after us? After Renato?*

"Sylvia and her sidekick will be waiting, probably with the police, maybe even Jacob, Canis, and Lee. I'll be arrested, or shot, and you'll be taken."

"She was at the hotel this evening," Heather told him. He looked at her with narrowed eyes. Heather added, "She said she wasn't ready to take us. She threatened your life," With this, Renato laughed comfortably. Heather explained to him about the scarf.

"Heather, I knew it. I tried to warn Hugh. I truly hate your mother."

"I know. I know that. I'm nothing like her."

His eyes warmed her. "No, nothing like her, Heather."

"I'm confused, Ren — why would my own mother kill Daddy?"

"She's crazy, and money hungry. She was mad at Old Man Whitney for being more powerful than her."

Heather stared off in search of peace. "In Savannah, I'm going to meet a man that will love me, that will show everybody I'm somebody."

"Interesting. You kiss me and dream about another?" Renato smiled.

"Well, you're the only man I've ever kissed," Heather gave a vague answer.

"So, you're already shopping around," Renato wanted to banter, or flirt.

"Well, you've kissed a lot of women, haven't you? Have you kissed Veronica?"

"Uh, yeah, but a long time ago."

"Lilac?"

He laughed, and answered, "Yes."

"Then your bootlegging days, sharing liquor and lips in all those speakeasies."

"Alright, . . . Alright, Heather. You made your point."

The truth was, as a nineteen-year-old that kissed one of the best-looking men around, Heather's heart was his clay, a thin clay that he couldn't do much with, but Heather was once again in a fragile state. Holding on to her dream of a singing and sweaty Black man in Savannah kept Heather from breaking.

"Savannah sounds alright to you?" Renato asked inquisitively. He knew the answer.

"It's exactly what I've been hoping for." They both stared out the window for a while at nothing but black night and the reflection of the empty seat in front of them. Renato huffed out a laugh and looked at Heather.

"Did I ever tell you about the moonshine steel with the bathwater gin?" He smiled eagerly at Heather, and something about being a playing piece in a game Heather wanted complete control over gave her the power to do exactly what she wanted. Heather placed her hands on Renato's cheeks, and she kissed him wholly. Renato kissed her back with his soft lips that — this time — were full of life and moved. Heather held his soft clammy cheeks in her hands, and they kissed.

Mae lay asleep on Renato's arm, and Renato rebalanced

Mae's sleeping head against his arm as Renato and Heather kissed. Mae awoke to Renato and stared at Heather and Renato in suspicion.

"Ren, did you just kiss me while I was sleeping?" Mae asked.

Renato laughed and answered, "No, Mae. I'm not as sneaky as you and your sister. You must have been dreaming about me."

The interior of the moving train was the safest they had been since leaving Sterling. No one else could get on. No one could threaten them. The other passengers minded their own. They were moving south, and for the time being, nothing could stop them. For the time being.

They knew that despite the peace provided in the Crow's Cart, it would eventually stop — the peace and the Crow's Cart. The present time was a moment they revered and hungrily lapped every second with the angst in the waiting room of their minds to come alive at the next train stop.

Heather opened her eyes in a startle. The flickering morning light heated through the train windows. The forest stopped and opened into rolling hills, lots of space, and rows of vegetables. Soon the land flattened out, resembling what Heather imagined to be Georgia. A silo stood ahead, and the train began to slow down. They weren't at the next station, just a work spot. Renato, Heather, and Mae were getting off here. Sylvia wouldn't be here.

Once the train stopped, most of the passengers stood up in unison to exit the cart. Renato, Heather, and Mae followed them onto dusty ground, out in the open. They were surrounded by factories and metal workshops, tall brick buildings, and a train station on down the tracks about a mile away. They stood and scanned their surroundings before they moved. The train rolled slowly away to the station. Several carts down the track, a group of trucks and a swarm of people exchanged crates, boxes, bags, and money. It was a new bustling day. Renato, Heather, and Mae kept their pace with the black working men, straight ahead, until they spotted a road.

They figured Sylvia and probably the police were on their way to the next station. A road lay out straight ahead, curving perpendicular to the railway. If the train was true south, they were walking east.

25

Run Boldly

They wanted to run, but they wanted to be unseen more. Their feet ignored the fire in them and stepped past a small wooden building, smaller than the lumber stack, then the engines, and then a tin-sided factory. The important bosses must have been in there, the way Black men kept walking in and out in a stooped-over, humble kind of way.

On the front of the building, a sign was posted: "Wanted!" with two drawings — a close-up of Renato, and another drawing of Mae and Heather. They were prey. Heather stopped and stared at the poster, feeling like she couldn't move.

"Heather," Renato instructed, "Heather, we gotta keep walking. We've got to get out of here."

A rumble of voices scattered all around them, piercing Heather's ears. They murmured incomprehensible demands.

"Has someone seen us?"

"I don't know."

"Is Momma at the train station yet?"

"I don't know."

"Who's waiting for us to get off the train?"

"I don't— how would I know?"

Sylvia saw them get on the night before, so she and her bow-tie friend may have gathered around that same green train cart they were just on, the one behind the engine.

"So, who does she want," Heather asked, "us or you, Renato?"

"Heather," Renato leaned in toward Heather, "come on! Please, please keep walking!"

They picked up the pace. Heather guessed someone had to have seen them get off early. Mae cried and spatted how this was crazy and why were they running from Momma. She'll surely understand. Heather was panting as they scuffled to reach the road. She couldn't speak. She felt a well of fear in her throat. Each step vulnerable to each second. The roadbed aligned thick with two-, three-, and four-story buildings, tired with broken hinges on shutters, hanging on wearily. Dusty windows hid their rooms inside. Weeds were long in tufts where there wasn't cement, and they erupted through cracks on the sidewalks. The town was imprinted with the Depression's fingerprints. Two cars passed by and the drivers paid them little attention. All was quiet. No one even walking. They paused at the corner of a tall brick building. Not a sound heard inside. The windows showed nothing but shaded space. Renato said they were somewhere in southern Tennessee, a "quiet town" which set on the Georgia line. He found it to be an introduction to the ugly parts of Georgia. Heather had not heard him speak of anything ugly about Georgia.

"Puttin' me on a 'Most Wanted' sign?" Renato questioned with a crack in his voice, dumbfounded. He turned around every few seconds to peer and to see if they were safe. "She got a manhunt to find me," Renato intensified his words, growing in anger.

"Ren—,"

Renato was panting as well. "Anybody— any person here might want to do good for their country . . . and shoot me. . . Not just Sylvia. You know? Not just Canis and Lee either. Not just the police. Anybody!"

"Ren, I think we've got to split up," Heather said. She tried to control the shake she felt in her voice.

"Heather, are we gonna get shot?" Mae asked.

"Any good . . . American . . . citizen," Renato added between breaths.

"Mae, nobody's gonna shoot you," Heather assured her. "Nobody is going to shoot any of us if we can stay level-headed!" Heather settled a glare on Renato.

Renato turned to study Heather and rested his face. "I'm sorry. Mae, no. I'll never let anyone hurt you. Especially Sylvia." Heather glared harder. *He didn't need to add Momma's name,* she thought. Mae broke into a full-blown cry.

"Momma would never hurt anybody!" Mae demanded. "Let's go somewhere! Instead of standing around huffing and puffing!"

Heather didn't have anything to run from; she could show the local police officers she was safe. Stop Momma's game. But too many what-ifs in Heather's head, like *what if she takes Mae from me? What if I don't see Renato again? What if I never make it to Savannah?* She resorted to think more about it once she saw Savannah. At that moment in the unknown town, Heather wanted to finish her dream.

"Ren, maybe we meet you two stations south, wherever that may be," Heather suggested.

Renato gave Heather a nod, rolled up his sleeves, and carried their luggage from the train with him. They walked towards a different block as Heather watched Renato stride away. Dread flooded Heather. She didn't feel any safer. She didn't know what else to do except move forward.

Heather pulled out a scarf and tied it around her head. Mae and Heather directed their steps down an empty alley to a road aligned with parked cars and several people. They found the life in the town, and Heather pierced her eyes through the crowd for a dark-headed Puerto Rican. She spotted suspenders like Renato wore, and she saw a hat similar to Renato's hat on a stranger's head. Down the sidewalk, a couple stood holding hands, and the back of the man favored Renato. Heather observed the man as they walked closer. The woman noticed Heather's stare. Within a few feet of the man, Heather noticed hair strands unmatched to Renato's. Heather observed his face as she passed, relieved the man was another stranger.

Where did he go?

Heather carried her purse tightly as she and Mae walked. They came to a restaurant door seeping out a wonderful smell of cooking. Mae swung open the door, and it burst out the smell of hot bread and butter and steaming meat. "Oh, my Lord!" Mae exclaimed, "I'm starving!"

They were stopped at the open door. Faces seemed everywhere, shooting looks at them, accompanied with a table of men shouting, "Nope! No! Troublemakers! Get out!" *Are they talking to me?* Heather stood confused.

"Yes! You! Get out!" a stout man aggressively shouted with clinched eyebrows, sitting on the edge of his chair, ready to get up and lunge Heather. Startled and scared, Heather and Mae scurried out.

"Heather," Mae pointed to a "Wanted!" sign posted in the diner. Heather quickly pushed her hand down. She was mortified! That man's hate pounded in her head. Reality was hard to ingest when it was uncomfortable. *How was he able to speak to me so proudly?* Heather wondered. They were hungry. *Do colored people not eat here? What do they do? Where do they go? No hunger pains trouble people here?*

Heather perceived others to know the limits of compassion. Limits must exist, but nobody told her. She had her own. She had limited compassion for Lilac Blanton, the foolish regular at Dodge Grocers. The only desperation she concealed was drool for Renato. Heather furthermore had little compassion for a woman who had money to buy and forget about a trunkful of clothes which fit Heather perfectly. She had no compassion for the dead murderer who shot her father. She'd let him starve, too. But Heather never killed anybody, and she was hungry.

She hoped Renato didn't see what just happened. She quickly combed her eyes through the streets and sidewalks outside. She walked down the sidewalk feeling like a coward, but she didn't know why. She tried to enjoy Mae's cussing. Mae had built up some anger for some time.

With the bus station across the street, they bolted down an alley to their right. Void of townspeople and humiliation, and fewer cars, they walked straight.

Mae mentioned, "Someone's gonna pass us and see us and think, 'Aren't those the two Negro girls on the "Wanted" signs?'"

The coming sounds of engines rumbled their missions past Heather and Mae, and they posed. Heather either pretended to pull weeds as if she lived at the house or building near her, or she tried to appear happy and unlost. As each motor grew in sound, her bones petrified. If a car stopped to question her, she'd be their prisoner. She couldn't have run. Each car kept up pace and passed by, and the motors grew fainter. A precious relief despite her thumping heart. They walked, not much poise left. Their feet ached and their throats were dry. Heather ignored the weakness set inside her body. Mae's curls formed a halo of frizz as she tried repeatedly to convince Heather to stop and surrender to "our loving Momma." That Heather should "give her a chance." That Heather was forcing her to live like a hobo when she could be living with Momma in the luxury of New York City. Heather contemplated telling Mae that Momma beat her and bruised her.

Killed Daddy.

How Momma was convincing that Heather pathetically existed and wasn't even worth the time of her mother. Perhaps Heather would never give Mae the full portrait of their Momma. Why remove ignorance if it kills a smile? Heather put up with Mae's pleas to protect her, even if it didn't make any sense to her.

Before getting to the outskirts of the city, Heather eyed the front page of the newspaper. It read,

"SYLVIA WASHER STILL IN FEAR!
'REYES KILLED MY HUSBAND!'"

Ironically, Heather smiled, but it quickly transformed into a cry.

"Heather!" Mae exclaimed. She placed her arms around Heather's waist and peered up at her. "Girl! Is this what falling in love is like?" *The absurdity!* Heather thought, but Mae got her to quit crying!

"What are you talking about?"

"You won't stop all this craziness, and it makes no sense, Heather!" Mae spoke with her eyes connected with Heather's. "It must be love. You know, I think I'm in love with Renato, too. Why else would I follow you everywhere? I guess we're both crazy in love."

"Mae" —

"And don't even say it, Heather!" She pointed her finger at Heather, giving her the most loving discipline she had ever received. "Don't even say it! Just shut up and let me sing." She pranced along in front of Heather and began the same song Heather had heard at least three other times since they left Sterling: *"We ain't got a barrel of money, Maybe we're ragged and funny; But we'll travel along, singin' a song, side by side."*

Mae was a gem. She wanted to shove out the worries Heather had about their Momma, but she couldn't. As Mae sang, Heather thought of Daddy.

"Don't know what's coming tomorrow; maybe it's trouble and sorrow, . . ."

Heather remembered, when she and Mae were much

younger and Sylvia was gone, Hugh told them a story about two mothers that went before the wise King Solomon.

"These two women came crying and fussing, and they tried tellin' the king they were the Momma of this one tiny, little child. 'I'm the Momma!' ... 'No! I'm the Momma!' That's what they'd both say. What do you think the king did?" Daddy asked Mae and Heather. Once Hugh confirmed his daughters' perplexed faces, he continued, "The king ruled to cut that baby in half and give each Momma an equal half. Sound fair?"

Mae and Heather gasped, "No!"

"Well, that's what he ruled!" Daddy claimed, "And the soldier come up and took the little baby, laid it out on a table, and lifted a sword, ready to chop that poor little baby right in half! But then, one of the mothers cried out 'No! Stop!' while the other mother cheered on the slaying, talking like, 'I'll take the bigger half!' Can you believe that?" Daddy shook his head. "If she couldn't have what she wanted, she thought no one could."

Heather thought of her mother. Some Mommas don't mind toying with their own child's life. Sylvia collected ammo, and Heather didn't know at what point her own survival would be Sylvia's target.

Heather and Mae walked for two hours. They held their shoes, and they hid or posed with every automobile that passed. They voiced their wonder of where Renato could be. Was Renato walking along the same path? Did someone pick him up in one of the passing automobiles? Heather stopped to smoke a couple of times. Mae smoked, too.

A wide, dark-brown building, the "Neighborhood Care

Center," didn't grab their attention. It was the backyard of the building, full of tents and people that pulled Heather and Mae closer. A real-life "Hooverville." Heather was just as desperate and hungry as anyone there. The "Wanted!" poster was bold on the front of the building. They walked to the side of the building straight to the slow-moving disarray of people in the back. Most tents were formed as teepees. Baggage for different families lay close to each tent. A couple of larger tents were set in the back of the community, furthest away from the care center building. Perhaps Renato stopped here as well. Some of the residents congregated and spoke together as if they had truly formed their own community, speaking in purposeful conversations, knitting and even laughing together. They had a few yards of a rectangle of dirt plowed and prepared for farming.

Something common was in the eyes of those depressed, like they'd seen something the rest of the Americans hadn't. Hugh once said every way of the Depression was contagious, and the Randolph family needed to be careful not to catch it.

But these people — they knew something. Strangely, Heather sensed a common knowledge of joy. They knew joy. They had seen it. And now it was gone and had been gone for some time. But they wanted it back and were restless for it. Joy was attainable, but not today, and probably not the next few days either. Maybe they were complainers, never satisfied, but Heather admired how they refused to never settle.

Heather approached a lady sitting on an upside-down bucket, knitting. "Good morning," Heather said, determined to not sound desperate. The lady pierced Heather's eyes with her own and froze them there. In a most ingenious way, she spoke to Heather with her eyes to tell her how her presence insulted her. Heather said nothing, and she and Mae walked on amid the camp. Heather spotted a group of Black people on one side of the yard. *My people!* Heather picked up her pace as if she had found her own family.

"Good morning," she approached a man and woman sitting on two small wooden benches outside the tents. They both looked at Heather with mouths opened and eyes opened wider. The lady must have been around Sylvia's age. Her skin was so black with creases and lines, it had to have been thick. A pink scarf was tied around her head and framed her twinkling eyes. Her black skin made her smile look brighter. The man wore overalls and stooped over to such a degree as if to say *Pay me no attention.* So, Heather didn't. They rolled their eyes to look at each other and smile. They knew who Heather and Mae were. Heather foolishly felt like a celebrity.

"Get in here and sit down, stupid girls!" the lady looked from side to side as she spoke, "Walkin' 'round like people ain't out lookin' fo' you two!" The lady, smiling, scurried Heather and Mae into their stuffy tent that had cots and a small table — surprisingly spacious. A little boy a few years older than Mae sat at the table. Heather explained how she and Mae weren't kidnapped. The lady said she knew already. Heather explained how she was desperate to see Savannah.

"Why you wanna go to Savannah? To get blacker? You wanna be hated even mo'? You don't know nothing 'bout the South, do ya'?"

Heather explained to her that her Daddy grew up in Savannah, and he had fond memories. The lady's belittling comments and stern stare mocked Heather's dreams.

"I know quite a lot more than most," Heather defended herself, "and the love of my life lives there."

"We lost him, though," Mae said. "We split up at the train."

Goodness, Mae!

"You mean to tell me the man that kidnapped you is the love of yo' life?" the woman asked and chuckled.

"No," Heather turned to Mae and stared hard at her for a solid second. The woman was Beatrice, and she knew Heather had a right to be scared to leave the tent. However, she didn't hide that she disapproved of the journey.

"What if he ain't there? Why you dependin' on somebody else for yo' happiness?" She placed her hands on her hips and stood over Heather.

"I'm independent," Heather cawed. "And maybe I'm just . . .bold."

"No, you ain't bold. But that's alright. We can't all be bold. Somebody's gotta hold the bold ones on a pedestal, or get stomped on by them."

After feeding Heather and Mae well enough, especially for a family living out of a tent, Beatrice coerced Mae into slipping on a pair of her son's overalls and his cap on her head. Mae looked like a fat Black boy. A black bean in overalls. Heather rolled a long, uncontrollable laugh. Mae and Beatrice laughed, too. Heather tidied up herself, and they left. Heather looked older, and Mae looked like a boy. Mae even exaggerated a boyish walk, mostly for fun so Heather would laugh again. Heather and Mae got comfortable, and they got bolder.

26

Destiny

They walked on a paved road for over three hours, in the countryside to the next neighborhood, and to the next town. Growing tired, hungry, thirsty, sore, particularly in their feet, Heather and Mae snapped at each other again and again.

A restaurant came into sight like a golden gate. Eastside Diner sat lonely, about the same size as Dodge Grocers, with a parking lot larger than needed. The door had a "Wanted!" poster with their pictures on it. Not caring, Heather opened the door, and a waitress stopped and looked at Heather. She wrinkled her eyebrows and tilted her head to the side.

"You're starving, aren't you? Come in," she pointed to a table in the corner. Only two other tables were taken, plus a few customers at the counter. A middle-aged gentleman sat at one table, and an older man and woman sat at the other. The atmosphere was subdued and quiet. Even the sunlight rays streaming beams of gold seemed to wish they'd never come in the diner. After having a seat, Heather spotted Renato sitting at the counter. Maybe he didn't know it was them. His plate of food was placed in front of him. Heather stared at him and scolded Mae when she kept turning around to see him. Heather lit a cigarette.

He looked uncomfortable as he ate. A large man sat two chairs down beside him and stared at him.

Renato looked straight ahead, trying to ignore the man's prolonged glances towards him. Renato turned his eyes to the man.

"I apologize for my bad table manners," Renato told him. "Obviously, I'm bothering you."

"No," the man answered. "It's not your manners I noticed, Jacob," his voice exaggerated its intonation. "It's the resemblance you have to the fella in that photograph."

Heather felt queasy. "I noticed that myself," Renato answered. "Too bad I don't have the two colored girls with me. Then I guess I'd be famous."

"Well, just what do you do, Mr. Jacob from Virginia?"

Renato looked straight ahead, "I'm not that guy."

"I think you are," the man responded.

Renato turned red and stiffened his jaw. "I don't want trouble. Do you?" he stared at the man.

"No, but I'm calling the police," he answered and got up. Heather's mind went into such a blur that she didn't notice where the man went.

Renato turned and spotted Heather and Mae. He stared for a moment, particularly at Mae. His startled expression turned into a smile and then a full-blown laugh. He strolled gallantly over to their table, like nothing was wrong, the same way he did when they were asked to get off the white bus in Illinois.

"Well, Miss," he leaned over their table and spoke towards Heather, then towards Mae, "and Sonny." They all laughed, and Heather felt sadness. "We can run, like this second and see how far we get before I'm shot. Or we can fold."

"Fold what?" Mae asked, "And where's our suitcases?"

"I had to let them go, Mae; I'm sorry. By fold I mean give up," Renato turned to the customers in the stores that had glued their eyes on Renato and Mae and Heather. "See? I didn't kidnap anybody." He slid into the seat next to Mae and pulled the cap off her head, staring at her and smiling.

"I'll be fine, Renato. I can make Momma love me. I make everybody love me," Mae said.

Renato stared at her, "I won't fight with you. It's true — you do seem to have a talent for stealing hearts." Renato kissed her forehead.

"So, it's over," I'll never see Savannah," Heather said.

"Not with me, Heather. Maybe one day in the future, when I've served my time, I can come home and see you and meet your sweaty black man," he smiled a smile so sad, Heather cried with a horrible feeling of defeat in her gut. Mae placed her head on Renato's arm. He grabbed Heather's hand and kissed it and held it to his cheek with his eyes closed.

"Heather, you remember when Hugh caught me giving you a shot of scotch?"

"I remember."

Renato chuckled, "You turned it up right when he walked

in the store." Then he laughed more.

"He was so angry with me," Heather said.

"Hugh was disappointed in me. . . I hated that. I let him down. And so, I promised him I would never do anything and that I would never let anyone hurt you. Ever." He gazed at Heather with a serious look. "I told him that because I never wanted to let you go, not because I was devoted to Hugh." Heather closed her eyes for a second. She thought of the live oak trees in Savannah that Renato said held old secrets.

Police cars pulled into the parking lot. Renato, Heather, and Mae didn't move.

"Renato, do you believe two lovers are destined to be together, even before they're born?" Heather asked.

"You mean like divine intervention? Or, like . . . maybe, divine manipulation?"

"Maybe just divine," Heather answered. Within a jumbled second, a police officer pointed a gun against Renato's head. Mae screamed.

"Not in front of the ladies. Please, be a gentleman," Renato calmly stated. Four police officers placed a grip on Renato and dragged him over the booth, knocking down tables, and out of the restaurant. They threw him on his stomach in the dirt in the front of the restaurant with the gun still pointed at his head. Several police cars sat in the front of the store. Mae continued to scream, escalating the bedlam. A crowd of people and cars stopped to join the panic in curiosity. The population quickly grew.

Soon, another car screeched in front of the diner. Sylvia got out with the bow tie man and a man with a camera. The camera man shot photo after photo as Sylvia ran with tiny steps. She wore a white boa and a shiny brown dress with a dark blue flower on the side of her head.

A woman in the restaurant said, "I'm just so happy for that poor mother!"

Ignorant input can be a fatal human flaw.

"My babies! My babies! . . . Where are they? Are they okay? . . . Did he hurt them? . . . Are they alive? Are they alive?" She shouted, obviously demanding attention.

"Momma!" Mae shouted back. Sylvia ran into the diner. Mae pulled herself out of the seat to hug her Momma. They embraced, and the hug was the first time they had ever held each other. It seemed the hug was fake, just for show, for attention. But it looked so real, like a mother and daughter should embrace. Heather thought her Momma might have changed and realized she needed to love her children and be their mother. But she sat still in the seat, not prepared to embrace Sylvia.

Heather looked out the window. Renato was staring at her, on his feet and handcuffed. By the time Heather met his eyes, he was turned around and shoved into the back of a police car. Police officers approached Sylvia, Heather, and Mae in the diner. They congratulated Sylvia. Hands were grasped and shaken throughout the diner in victory. Mae had her picture taken with Sylvia. Heather sat, and the photographer shot the camera in her face.

Sylvia shimmied her high heels outside to the police car. She blared towards Renato, "You should be hanged!" A sloppy applause from the onlookers approved her victory cry.

"So should you," Heather whispered. Sylvia shuffled back in the restaurant basking in the attention. She lit a cigarette and stood over the table where Mae and Heather sat.

"We're gettin' out of here. Let's go," Sylvia leaned over the table, "We're headed to Savannah for a quick minute!" Sylvia squeaked. Heather slid her cigarette case off the table, the one she took from her in the speakeasy.

"Not quite yet, ma'am," an officer told her. "We need to question your daughters at the police station. We'll show you a place to stay for you and the girls."

"To stay? What, a hotel?" Sylvia asked, "How long have I got to stay?" She stood up straight with a hand on her hip. He glanced at Heather's lack of gratitude as she lounged back with her arms folded.

"Just a night," he answered.

"Why are we going to Savannah?" Heather looked up and asked Sylvia. She ignored Heather, so she asked again.

"Heather!" Sylvia snapped at her and then remembered to smile, "We just have to pick something up. A real quick errand."

"Pick up what?" Heather asked. Momma looked irritated with Heather.

"You nosy girl!" Sylvia whispered.

"Woman, Momma. I'm a nosy woman." The waitress brought Heather and Mae glasses of water. They grabbed their waters and gulped.

"Quit stealing my cigarettes!" She held out her hand for her smokes.

"Why are we going to Savannah?" Heather enunciated.

"Heather!" Mae started, "Calm down!" Momma slipped in the booth next to Mae and leaned over closer to Heather.

"Heather," she started, "to get the deed. The deed to the

store. Some Mr. Haverson man has it, is what Mrs. Whitney told me. And you're going with me, Miss Woman! I need you to sign it over to me," Sylvia said. "And if you don't," she leaned over closer towards Heather and whispered, "you'll regret it." She backed up and continued staring at Heather. "Renato will most likely be shot dead by the end of the day. You know that, right?" She stared at Heather. She knew Heather cared.

Small groups huddled throughout the diner and the parking lot. Excitement was in the air. It was on their faces. Each group turned to look at the three ladies reunited at last. Then back to sharing what they thought. What they knew.

"You gonna shoot Renato, Momma?" Mae asked.

"Not me, no, but he made a lot of his mobster friends angry for pulling them into this mess! I bet they all want to take turns blowing his head off!" she declared with a victorious smile waving her hand in the air like she was a conductor of misery. The long-winded woman exhaled on: Renato kidnapped. Renato stole from the store. Renato, the Puerto Rican bootlegger.

"No, he didn't."

"Who didn't what, Heather?" Sylvia asked.

"I did all this. I let Renato take the fall for it, and he let me."

"If he lives, Renato's going to prison!" Sylvia said.

The sun hid behind dense trees across the street, as it should have for teasing Heather. The police car holding Renato drove away. People hollered at it.

"Rot in jail!"

"Mobster!"

"Bootlegger!"

"Go back to Puerto Rico!"

Heather slipped away to an officer who looked around everywhere but at Heather. He assured Heather she'd get a chance to speak. The officer asked the townsfolk to commence their day. Heather stood beside him and found it a challenge to swallow, and she remembered Doris's words: "Nobody's ever gonna give you permission to speak!"

"I need to know when, please, sir. I have to speak."

"You'll be questioned in the morning. Go to the motel with your mother," the officer instructed.

It looked like the way to freedom was by getting in bow tie man's car with Mae and her mother. They followed a police car to a motel in Dalton, Georgia. Mae and Heather sat blindly like two scared peons in the back seat as Bow Tie Man and Sylvia sat in the front. They didn't turn to look at Heather and Mae or speak to them. They didn't even speak to each other. The Chattanooga jail was full, so Renato had to be held in Dalton, Georgia — further south. How lucky Heather should have felt.

Further south.

Good luck is a tease to hope.

27

Secrets and Jail

Georgia held secrets. It was sectioned with walls of dense trees, sometimes closing in the sky. Distance couldn't be seen. Open spaces spattered tall, skinny trees with no consistency, like it wasn't prepared to disclose.

The motel was a boring brown brick rectangle, transparent of the woes of guests who had come in and out. The four of them had one room to stay in, all four of them together. Luckily, Bow-tie Man paid for a second room. Heather still didn't know his name, and she didn't care to ask.

An officer pulled up into the hotel parking lot and gave Heather and Mae their luggage which was found in southern Tennessee close to the railroad where Renato left them. Outside the motel was unwelcoming air, insignificance. Heather felt the air pushing her although there was no wind. Heavy dampness attempted to crowd her out of Georgia.

Heather remembered her father saying, "Illinois is where they hide their hearts but freely expose their actions. Georgia is where they hide their actions but freely expose their hearts."

Even in the air, this was true. Heather once could feel the Illinois western winds moving, approaching from the dusty fields, and diving deep into her chest, trying to pull out whatever stirred inside, no matter what shame or darkness was in there. But Heather moved on and ignored it.

In Georgia, Heather wondered of its contents, her hate for her Momma, her resentment for Mae, her brokenness for her Daddy, and her passion for Renato. All her life was out of place and out of balance. She responded in haste to keep all these deceptive wiles bound. It didn't seem reasonable to showcase adulation nor sorrow, not here in Georgia.

The officer advised they'd be picked up the next morning and taken to the jail house for questioning.

"Please come early," Heather begged the officer.

She lay in bed that night and tried to entertain every thought of leaving the motel and finding Renato. But the long day of walks and the arrest tranced her asleep quickly.

The next morning, Heather dressed quickly in the dark one-room motel room. Mae slept. Heather opened the door to a dark morning and walked the direction she saw the police officer leave the previous night. She hoped it was towards Renato. The dark walk on the strange road did not intimidate Heather; she was no amateur at walking roads. Headlights came towards her. A police car stopped and ordered her in the car.

"He's still alive?" Heather asked. The officer glared at her and gave no answer.

Upon arriving at the police station, Heather begged for a

visit with Renato. Considering they were waiting on the detective to show up, she was allowed to see him. An officer escorted Heather down a hallway to the back. The last cell was Renato's. Renato smiled and laughed. His sleeves were down, his suspenders swayed by his sides, and his hands were in his pockets as he ambled around the small space. Heather stood tall, practically at allegiance, beaming that he stood and breathed. She pulled a wooden chair sitting at the end of the hall by Renato's cell and sat.

"Buenos días! How'd you get back here?" he asked.

"What's going to happen?" Heather whispered as if too painful to speak.

"I don't know," he answered. Heather felt like a battle-stricken soldier on the brink of being wounded, of dying. Renato stood relaxed. Heather's angst increased.

"You okay?" he asked.

"No, Ren. You're in jail and I'm with Momma."

"Yeah, it makes sense though." He pulled up a chair in his cell and sat facing Heather. "This Depression and everything, it's really bad."

"Ren, I know," Heather answered.

"In all of it, though," he continued, "you know, it hasn't hit me."

Heather knew this as well. If the Depression arose without the Prohibition, this may have concocted Renato a different life story. But he made several contacts and connections with all the speakeasies running north and south. He made money, easy money. If alcohol was legal, he'd be poor.

Renato continued, "You know, bootleggers are arrested

and shot all around me. All the time. I live in depression, you know, just differently."

He slouched in the small chair, surrendered to this moment and the next.

"You remember the people at the barn after the tornado?" he asked, "And they weren't bootleggers. I wished I was like them." His eyes smiled at Heather. "They had misfortunes, and they never deserved it." Others tried, worked hard, had real jobs, and lost everything. Still, tomorrow was no guarantee for anyone. Renato's face saddened and his eyes darkened. "And then, you look at me. My misfortunes? You know, all . . . this. I deserve it. And really, you know? But that's my life."

Renato's fortunes were not conventional, if blessings could be scaled. They were different. The same with his misfortunes.

He added, "Heather, I'm fine." His face and eyes were relaxed as he looked at Heather. "I probably won't change my life, and I won't complain about this. I'm glad we're here. I mean, I liked Sterling. They loved us, you know? But I'm glad we're here."

"Yes, I suppose you'd still be liquoring up Lilac," Heather jested, despite her tear-stained face. Renato smiled.

He answered, "I don't think so. You were mad at me about that! I knew it!" They sat quietly for a while.

"How long until we see Savannah?" Heather asked Renato. She managed a smile to pair with her hopelessness.

"It's about a whole day's trip," he answered with no enthusiasm. Heather could tell he had no hopes of seeing Savannah or even seeing the end of the day. On a bleak day, no one notices if the sky is blue.

"I once inquired about traveling to Puerto Rico," he shared. A distressing thought for Heather, losing Renato again.

"I asked a lady working on a port off River Street downtown. And she said, 'The distance between Puerto Rico and the coast of Brunswick, Georgia, is about 1100 nautical miles. *Nautical* miles.' So, I asked her, 'Nautical miles? What's the difference?' and she answered, 'It's on water.' . . . What?" He chuckled and looked at Heather, waiting for a laugh. Heather smiled.

Quick footsteps and a man's silhouette carried a briefcase as boring as the man's entrance. He walked to them, pulled up a chair, and introduced himself as Barnabas Hughes, Renato's public defender. No smile as he glanced at Heather and pulled a folder out of his portmanteau. The lack of a hat over his inconsistent curls elevated Heather's distrust in the man. His rounded-rim glasses were too big for his pointy face.

"Fifty years to life," he spat out with a closed smile, a smile similar to Mrs. Hawk's. He kept going, "That's what the District Attorney is offering. I don't see how you're getting out of this mess. Where were you headed anyway?"

Heather and Renato didn't move. Renato glanced at Heather with worry in his eyes. Heather felt her body taking the number fifty like poison, turning her blood to stone. Heather wondered if Mr. Hughes was also a member of the Anti-Saloon League. She noticed a shiny silver pen with black engraving of something she couldn't make out. She wondered if Mae was out of bed, if her mother checked on Mae. Her mind sprinted through thoughts in divided seconds.

Something bad was swelling in Heather's chest.

Renato calmly answered, still slouched in his chair, "Savannah, or Brunswick, to my family."

"Stealing some slaves along the way?"

"Hell, no," Renato answered. A venom ignited in Heather. She didn't want to be pushed down anymore.

"I can speak for myself," Heather intervened. "You can see me sitting here, can't you?"

"I'm on your side," answered the attorney.

"Such a simple mindset," Heather carried on, "so sure that us colored girls have no other use but to be slaves."

"Well, it's a charge, along with robbery, theft, breaking and entering, illegal transport of alcohol, illegal sales of alcohol, illegal use of alcohol, attempted murder in Oglesby, possibly Pittsburgh and Sterling, . . . apparently. . . Let's see, . ." He looked through his stack of papers. "Did you try to steal a car in Oglesby?"

"Now you're making things up," Renato answered and leaned closer to the bars towards the attorney. "You're my attorney or my executioner? I'm confused."

"You're our country's most wanted. Prison is your new home, probably forever," he remarked. "And, seemingly, the government doesn't like your friends. I'm just telling you what you're up against. You'd like me to sugar-coat it?"

Renato laughed. "Are you serious? The government loves my friends. My friends bend the government over all the time; the government loves it!" Renato mumbled in Spanish and added in a heated shout, "What do you know?" Heather hated Renato's tone, but she understood it.

"Fifty years to life. That's what I know," Mr. Hughes

answered. He stuffed the folder back in his bag and stood up. "We'll talk, since it's my job."

"I need to speak with you, now," Heather said and stood with Mr. Hughes. She felt life and hope back in her body. He stared at her with doubt but agreed to sit in a separate room with an officer and Heather. The detective entered behind them. The attorney and the detective probed Heather for answers, mostly dealing with alcohol, speakeasies, and the dead and living "organized crime partners."

"And the store in Sterling, Dodge Grocers — it was burglarized."

"Momma stole the money." Heather felt cheap speaking lowly of her own mother, but only for a passing moment. She told them about the scarf with the blue flower when her father was killed. She gave details about Sylvia's beatings.

"Children get beat, Miss Randolph," they explained.

"We ran away. I begged Renato to let us tag along with him." That was closer to the truth.

"That doesn't make this any better. Children can't just run away with a grown man. Renato is still accountable," they answered. The men saw Heather as a vulnerable girl, swooned by Renato's charm.

"I am nineteen; I'm not a child! I can go wherever I want to go. I'm also old enough to take care of my sister when she doesn't have a mother willing to be a mother!" Heather's voice elevated. "I did nothing wrong!"

"Even grow affections for their kidnapper. Feelings for him."

"What? I . . . No. He's a family friend!"

"Children — sometimes even young adults as yourself —

are supposed to stay with their mothers, Miss Randolph."

"I thought Southern businessmen didn't let colored children stay with their parents!" With this they narrowed their eyes to Heather, then spoke with each other. They again asked what Heather knew about alcohol distribution, organized crime, any speakeasies she knew about.

"What are we doing here?" They spoke with one another. "New charges?" . . . "amend the kidnapping charges?" . . . They stuffed their words of thoughts and solutions in the meeting for over an hour. Heather worried about Mae. Was she still asleep? Would Sylvia be mean to her?

The defense attorney gave her a sheet of paper and a pen to write a statement of Heather's certainties. She wrote with his shiny silver pen. She held it in her hand and tried to place it in her lap under the table before he asked for it.

"Miss Randolph, thank you for your time. Renato has several charges to answer to, but you did help. Our officer will drive you back to the motel. We'll need to speak with your sister Mae Randolph and to your mother. If that's everything, have a good day."

Heather felt like a puppet. They allowed her to go back to the cell to tell Renato goodbye while they prepared a ride for her back to the motel. She relayed the information to Renato. He sat quietly for a while.

"So, can you try to have some hope, Renato?" Heather asked.

He smiled and gazed at Heather.

"This is it, Heather, and it's okay. It's all okay," Renato said. "One more thing— can I tell you something? I wanted to kiss you, too," he said. Heather sensed a sadness. He kept

on, "I'd just shout, 'Adiós! . . . Bye, Heather,' and you'd
answer me sweetly. Beautiful voice. My heart perked, like,
really felt it when you spoke. I walked back to my house, and
I thought, 'dulce como un beso' - sweet as a kiss. It had to be."
He held the bars and leaned his face closer in between them,
seemingly hoping Heather would kiss him.

Heather sat back in the chair. She didn't kiss him back.
She regretted it later, but the angst within her clouded over
sharing sentiments with Renato. Besides, kissing often meant
goodbye or bad things were coming.

Down the hallway, they heard the door of the jail house
squeak open. Renato and Heather both paused to listen to a
voice with an authoritative tone, all muffled. A set of shoes
clopped down the hall towards them. An officer set a chair
beside Heather, and a man in a stiff suit that exalted wealth
sat down.

"Renato," the man situated his overcoat to assure his
authoritative pose. "Renato, you look like hell. Do they let you
shower down here?" The man looked around as if searching
for a lavatory attendant. *He's worried about Renato's hygiene?*
Heather was curious.

"No, not yet," Renato answered shortly with no interest
in being his host.

"You wanna' get a shower? Let's go. . . Guard! Let's go,"
he stood up, and Heather did as well. "Get the man a
shower!" He looked back at Renato, "I got a suit for you. Go
shower, for Christ's sake. Now sit down. We need to talk."
They all three sat back down at his command. Heather was
confused. He looked over at her and asked, "Who are you?"

"I- I, I'm Heather Randolph."

"I thought the Randolph girls were young. You're a woman," he wrinkled his eyebrows and looked at Renato.

"Yeah, you're right," Renato answered.

"Oh, I see," the man looked at Renato with a slight smile. Renato looked perturbed.

"Explains everything," he turned back to Heather. He cordially asked her to leave him to "speak business" with Renato and for Heather to speak to Sylvia about dropping the charges.

Are you going to kill Renato? Heather wondered as she stood to leave. He began his conversation before she walked down the hallway.

"You've been one of my few true friends, am I right, Renato? So watch out! The feds are on Chicago just like in Savannah. So watch out!" His eyes rested solid and wide on Renato, and he pointed his fat, tan finger. "Isaac, your brother, he better watch out! I've always loved you and your family. You know that, right? No one can argue with that." The man turned to stare at Heather with a blank, unsmiling stare, he refrained from speaking until she walked away. She didn't turn to look at Renato. Or to say goodbye. She slid out the door and kept walking until she was outside. Heather was free.

No one was around to tell her "let's go," or "New York." No one to follow or hear. She stood still in front of the jail house, and she wanted to stay there forever, in this free spot. Would forward be free? To Mae. Back to Mae. Forward to Mae. Where's freedom in love? She didn't want to see Mae, nor Sylvia, nor Renato. So, she walked the opposite way from the motel. Heather walked South. She was hungry and thirsty and alone and free.

She heard the revving of a police car as she walked toward the peak of a hill. The car drove her way. Heather wanted to get to the peak. *What was on the other side?* She couldn't see. The motor was rattling in her head. It clunked slower and stopped beside her. She stared at the peak, but she had to stop.

"Miss, you're walking in the wrong direction," the officer hollered out the window. "The motel is the other way. Get in the car. I'll take you back." Heather hesitated before climbing in. He drove to the top of the hill to turn around. Heather saw the other side — more road.

The officer offered her a cigarette and drove down the endless, straight road towards the motel. Mae needed Heather, whether she thought so or not.

Keep your mind on Mae, Heather. Mae needs you now. Time to return. Back. Back. Back.

The cigarette was helpful. Georgia had a big sky. The officer was young, maybe around Renato's age. Heather wasn't going to cry. Who was that man in the suit, acting as if he owned Renato? He never told his name. Heather wished she would have kissed Renato. She loathed the ride to the motel, back to a starting pit. But she had to. Mae was there. Heather needed Mae. Her pretty clothes were there. Sylvia may have had a few things and some cigarettes she could steal. Stealing from Sylvia might help her feel better. She had to get there.

28

New Dreams

What happens when someone dreams outside the world of their loved ones? Drop their dreams? And what was right and fair to Mae? She wanted to be with her mother. She did dream of love, and of keeping it.

Heather knocked on the door of the motel. The officer accompanied her in order to take Mae to the station for questioning. Mae answered, looking bewildered, but trying to mask it with happiness. She was cleaned up and dressed, putting on her shoes.

"What's going on?" Heather asked as she walked in. The room was empty.

"Momma said when you got back, she wants you to come visit her. She said she's missed you, Heather!" Mae looked at Heather with anticipation.

"Hmmm, alright," Heather walked towards the door, "You coming?"

"No," Mae shook her head. Something was bothering her. "Momma said I couldn't come back in her room till I took a shower and tried to make myself look better." Mae looked hurt. The officer instructed Mae to leave with him.

"Mae, did she hurt you?" Heather asked as they walked to the car.

Mae wrinkled her nose in disappointment and shouted, "No!" Heather walked to Sylvia's room. Sylvia opened the door. It was dark inside besides the morning's cloudy white light peering in through the rectangular window's half-opened curtains. The light magnified the tippet of dust down the edges of the curtains.

"Where've you been?" Sylvia demanded.

"Where do you think?" Heather responded just as curtly. Sylvia held up her hands and closed her eyes as if trying to control her anxiety.

"What'd you say?" she asked.

"A mafia man showed up. He told me to tell you that you better make the charges go away." Heather stood in front of one of the curtains.

Sylvia stared and blinked as if in horror, and Heather felt sorry for her. What an ambiguous feeling; surely Heather would never doubt again that Sylvia was a terrible mother. Not even a mother to Heather anymore. Heather hoped she'd never ease up on her mother again, but she probably would. That was the deep-rooted fear — she'd give her mother another chance. And another, and another. This was the reasonable course of life between a mother and a child, no matter how old the child. Sylvia was the provider of life, and Heather was programmed to believe her. Despite how harsh Sylvia was or how abandoned Heather felt, Sylvia was never completely wrong, and Heather would always keep the door open to give her another chance. It was terrifying.

"I'm not gonna do that," Sylvia said, "Mae. She respects me, Heather. She respects her mother!" Sylvia sat on the bed and strained as she spoke, "I haven't had much respect come my way, I don't know why. I'm not a likeable kinda person. But now, I sing and I see people with this- this affection on their faces. You know, I got hundreds of people loving me, loving my singing, and you — my own girl — you look at me like I'm . . .!" She had a loss for thinking of something. She glared at Heather and whispered, "How dare you!

"I tried," she nodded her head, "I know I tried. Yes, . . . I did! I know I did; you and your father knew I did. You and Mae, you sucked the life out of me. I gave you two everything. Everything I knew to give you. Why can't I have everything, Heather? Why? Singing made me happy. What, I couldn't be happy? I tried to make a better life for myself, and you acted like I couldn't be your Momma anymore. Renato humiliated me every time I'd come around. So, you tell me, Heather — why would I want to come home anymore? Why would I want to see you? You disgusted me."

"Where's the deed, Heather?" the strange bow-tie man asked. He stood in the way of the door and Heather.

"I don't know. I don't — I don't know," Heather answered in apprehension, startled with the man's sudden appearance and presence in the room of intimate conversation. Also, he wasn't wearing his bow tie; Heather didn't want to know him that well.

"The police called this morning before you got back. They want to speak to me. Why the hell would they want to speak to me?" Sylvia asked, staring at Heather.

"Who was the man that killed Daddy, Momma?" Heather asked and continued to stand in front of the curtain. She wished she could keep taking steps backwards. Momma turned to look down with a deep breath, then back at Heather.

"We're going to Atlanta to stay for a little while," she said. "I'm out of money. I'll perform, and you'll get a job, you and Mae."

"In Atlanta?"

"Yes, Heather. In Atlanta. We don't have the money to get to Savannah."

"I got an apartment," the man said, "but you have to pay for your keep. You'll sleep outside after a beating if you don't."

"Oh, Benny," Sylvia whispered, "sounds too beasty." Heather sensed chagrin; Sylvia narrowed her eyes at Heather and added, "Then, we're going for the deed. Your father put it in your name to humiliate me."

Heather was told to pack. Mae returned shortly after, excited to enter into a world with her mother. Sylvia and Benny left to be questioned. Heather could practically see the dreams circling in a jovial cloud over Mae's head as they prepared to leave.

Heather thought of tall marsh as she packed in the motel room. She thought that if she could stand in the marsh, she would. When their mother returned, Mae met Sylvia and Benny at the car. With the motel room lights out, Heather sat on the bed, thinking she would cry. Heather's eyes soon adjusted to the darkness.

Benny came into the room, stood at the door and said, "Your friend Renato is dead. . .

"Shot in the jail. . .

"Right in the head." He stared at Heather with every new statement, enjoying the pain he gave her. Heather felt nauseous. Her nose stopped up, and she could hardly breathe. Her face was coated with tears. It throbbed, but the inability to breathe took her whole focus. She washed her face and wept. She cursed herself for creating this whole journey.

She didn't tell Mae. She couldn't get out the words. She sat by Mae in the back seat and stared out the window in horror. *Renato is gone! He's gone!*

They passed the jail. Heather saw it like a tombstone belonging to Renato. She didn't hold in her weeping, and she folded over in the seat. Sylvia and Mae were speaking, but Heather couldn't hear their words. Mae scooted closer to Heather to hug her. Heather sat up and gazed out the window.

"Heather," Sylvia started, "Quit thinking about that dead man. Your dreams are crazier than mine." She laughed towards Benny, and he obliged.

The new family headed south to Atlanta.

29

A New Life

tlanta, Georgia, had a personality that stood tall and didn't care if you were staring or not, but what a loss not to. Steps of the people were slower amidst every busy day with less worry of whether or not a destination would be seen. With a closer look, you'd see a hesitation between each step that contained unnoticeable moments of dreams and dismays, and then they kept going. Massive brick buildings claimed corners of blocks and kept tenants tucked in, unless they propped their doors opened with a table covered with whatever they could find in hopes passerby's might make a purchase. And Atlanta was glutton for decor of any kind, in red, bold words on a tin sign caked with dust, or a fancy awning with frayed hems dancing with a breeze from a passing bus or truck, or a painted outdoor cement wall where someone was willing to take what they had and make it look pretty.

The family's two-room apartment was reached by climbing outdoor metal stairs. There was also an indoor staircase, but the eighth and ninth steps were gone, and the metal stairwell allowed them to be outside quicker. One room contained a mattress where Benny and Sylvia slept, and the front room contained an icebox, a sink, a small burner, and a skinny mattress where Mae and Heather slept together. A mirror, mottled with black spots, stared at them from over the sink. Four other dark gray, three-story apartments invited the bad luck and the hard knocks. Their family lived on the second floor of Building B.

Heather learned of a spot near a home maintenance store on Lakewood Avenue where Black women stood ready to be hired as domestic helpers. A groomed woman in her 30's, and of Southern stability in a stylish hat and a rusty-colored dress, walked into the store, studying Heather on her way in. After some time, she approached Heather when she came back out.

"Are you in need of work?" the woman asked Heather.

"Yes, ma'am," Heather answered truthfully, accepting the fact.

Heather walked with the lady through the bustling city, straight ahead until the density of people was no more. Mrs. Griffin, as the woman introduced herself, explained Heather's duties in the Griffin home as they walked swiftly.

The Griffin family lived in a dainty white and green antebellum home that sat several steps up from the main sidewalk. They resided on the same road as Heather, two miles down.

Heather walked to the home each morning and noticed the transformation in scenery. From Heather's apartment, she smelled aches and fatigue, musty dread and mold; she passed buildings built so close beside one another, the alleys between them were used as homes for a few people. Buses, trucks, and unending rattles of cars left traces of gas smells. A scream came from all ages at all times.

She kept walking. Bushes began to line the sidewalk, and if Heather listened closely enough, she heard birds sing. When Heather passed the first home lined with manicured bushes, a cozy front porch, and a serene courtyard, she acknowledged a new ambiance of those with sturdiness, those who caught all the best graces thrown out.

The Griffin children called her Miss Heather, and they prepared to know her at no endpoint.

"Miss Heather, play with us."

"Miss Heather, may we style one another's hair?"

"Miss Heather, where do you live?"

The expectation of family, or friendship made Miss Heather sigh and sometimes tear. The children had dreams, too, but Heather didn't want to hear them. She kept most of her attention on preparing each meal for the family.

"Miss Heather, are you married?" Caroline, the ten-year-old, once asked.

"No, not yet."

"Oh, are you gonna get married?"

"Yes."

"Oh, Miss Heather! When? Soon?"

"Yes."

"But, you won't leave us, will you?"

"A part of everyone's dream is to leave, Caroline."

Heather's money from Dodge Grocers disappeared once

they were settled in their apartment. Neither her mother nor Benny took it, Heather concluded, considering they were still stressed over their lack of funds. Heather was determined to save her money until she could find another dream, or rather allow a dream to find her; she was too tired to look for one anymore.

Mae's delightful curls expired into one ball of dull frizz. She didn't care to look in the mirror as often as she once did. Her full cheeks held grieving eyes, and she didn't sing as often. She tried and tried to sing with her mother when they first settled in Atlanta, and Sylvia responded with "Please, enough." Mae was sent out every morning to find a job, and she hated Georgia. A woman with a thick accent slapped Mae one morning. Mae claimed she couldn't understand the woman.

"She spoke like she was drunk, like she was about to sing, but it sounded bad, so she spoke. So, I said something, and she slapped me." Atlanta hadn't yet learned of the treasure of being in the presence of Mae Randolph. She came home daily with nothing but a bland self-perception.

The Griffins wouldn't allow Heather to bring her sister, but they often sent Heather home with extra food for Mae.

Sylvia and Benny visited the bars and speakeasies in the area. They typically kept their daily lives separate from Heather and Mae. Sylvia mentioned leaving for Savannah and finding the deed repeatedly.

"Real soon," she said one evening as she left. Heather sat on the metal steps and watched her mother and Benny walk away through the street in front of their complex. People meandered east and west, most of them done with obligations of the day. Automobiles kept a steady roll; pedestrians repurposed the road into an expanded sidewalk.

She noticed a man walking with a saxophone. He wore a dark blue coat and a bow tie. Although he had to have been going to work, he panted as if exhausted. Heather suspected he performed at a speakeasy. He didn't smile, and his eyebrows were wrinkled as if he was angry. A rickshaw cart came racing by pulled by a boy about Mae's age. The side of the cart bumped the saxophone player, causing him to straggle his steps. He grasped his saxophone with both hands and held it to his chest like a child. The man belted out a roaring shout that stopped the boy pulling the cart. The man held his saxophone over his head to strike the boy. The boy cowered and bowed his back, preparing to be hit.

"Hey!" A woman on the third floor shouted. The man and the boy paused and found the source of the voice standing on the metal steps, just over Heather. The man began walking on, glaring with hate at the woman. As he came closer, she noticed beads of sweat over his dark skin, a slightly different shade from her own father's. The boy took the moment to run away with his cart. Heather glared with equal anger at the man.

Indignation swelled within her. She stood where she didn't want to, staring down at a man wearing undignified sweat. And she missed Renato. She now had Mae, and she had the Griffins, she supposed.

She had no right to find her job onerous, but she looked around every day at what she didn't have - Renato. And what she couldn't have. She didn't feel like taking anything from the Griffins. She had no pull to do so. So, she never stole anything from them.

She confided in Mrs. Griffin how she used to take things, but she promised never to take anything from them. Heather revealed many things to Mrs. Griffin. Mrs. Griffin encouraged her honesty.

"Miss Heather, would you like a shot of scotch?" Mrs. Griffin once asked.

"No, no ma'am. I'm working."

"Well, I see your eyes shifting to the bottle, so do you want a drink?"

"I'm sorry. No ma'am."

"No? Well, I look at the bottle from time to time myself and think, perhaps I shouldn't, but if we're both thinking that, perhaps we should have one and get it out of the way."

"Are you sure, Mrs. Griffin — I'm working."

"So am I, Miss Heather. It's my house and my children and my servants. Mr. Griffin is never here, so oh my, so much work." She poured two shot glasses full of scotch for her and Heather.

Mrs. Griffin was often home alone; Heather had seen Mr. Griffin at home only once.

Mrs. Griffin once observed Heather staring admiringly at her brass teaspoons which were engraved with dainty loops, inflaming the shine and regalia of the small objects.

"Place one in your pocket, Heather. I have too many," Mrs. Griffin quietly spoke, conveying they were sharing a secret. Her kindness made Heather sad knowing she had to leave her.

"Mrs. Griffin," Heather spoke lowly in return, "I have dreams."

Mrs. Griffin batted her lashes and answered, "How sad. I'm sorry."

Heather walked home with the assigned sorrow, and she remembered her age as a grown woman with bitterness, but forgot how to step forward as a grown woman. The night sky darkened quickly, and two couples walked down the opposite side of the road. They were dressed for a party, ruffles, shines, and shimmers as sparkling as the laughter. She wondered if they were going to a speakeasy to dance, like she did. They glanced over at Heather and continued on their gallant way. And she decided to remember.

Heather propped against a waist-high stone wall. She stared at the empty road reflecting the streetlight. She pictured herself wearing the black sequined dress with her hair done by Doris, walking into the middle of the road. On the side of the road was Renato with his hands in his pockets, staring at her. He waltzed casually and calmly with the well-known Renato charm that drove Sterling girls crazy. He took her hand and slid his other arm around her waist. And they danced. Heather soaked in the dream until an automobile's lights beamed directly on her as it drove by. The dream was over, but she felt as if she had just finished dancing with Renato.

The next morning, Heather took a side road to the post office before her work.

"Can you help me find a family in Savannah?" Heather asked the clerk.

The clerk stared at her for a moment, then asked, "Last name?"

"Reyes-Sanchez."

The clerk requested two days to find the family. Heather also asked for some paper and a pen, and she didn't allow the clerk's acrimony to pull her to regression. While at the post office, she wrote a letter to Isaac, Renato's brother. She held on to the letter walking back to the apartment, and as she ate bread with Mae. She slept with the letter, and she felt lighter in her steps on her morning walk to the Griffins.

She returned to the apartment that evening, and Sylvia accosted her regarding pay.

"The store burned down. Dodge Grocers, it's . . . It's gone," Heather told her mother.

"What! Wait, girl, where'd you hear this?" Sylvia asked. Benny came from the back room to hear.

"I got a letter from Mrs. Whitney. She said so," Heather felt invincible in her planned lies.

"Letter? What damn letter?" Sylvia shouted.

"Let me see it!" Benny followed.

"I threw it away on the way home. I was so upset crying," Heather managed a most solemn face which was not completely fabricated. "The store. My store. Gone. Everything. Gone."

Mae cried and wailed how she missed her Daddy. Heather let her. Mae needed to grieve without the facade of her mother's love, this fantasy future.

Sylvia and Benny shuffled their feet this way and that in confusion as they prepared and puffed and prettied for the evening. Both of them dumbfounded. They did not return late that night as usual, nor the next morning. Nor the next few mornings.

After two days, Heather returned to the post office to

receive a Savannah address, and the letter was mailed. When she returned from the post office, she told Mae she lied about Dodge Grocers. Mae's eyes smiled for the first time in Georgia.

"Let's go see it!" Mae beamed. Heather felt the burden again of making Mae happy. Why couldn't they walk in the same direction to happiness?

"Mae, I promise one day I'll take you back up to Sterling, but I need you to trust me that I can take care of you and make you happy."

Ten more days passed, and Heather left each morning to her duties at the Griffin home. The children, Caroline, John, Eva, and Elmer, expected each morning to be awakened by the soft voice of Heather, to be hugged by her as if she'd never get a chance to hug them again. Their appreciative little arms hugged her back, with less understanding of it being their last.

The family, including Mr. Hughes, left for an outing and Miss Heather's services wouldn't be needed that day. Heather dressed the children in thick cotton and velvet and left late in the morning. She walked home with a whirl of anticipation that rooted deeply and grew relentlessly every day. She walked the familiar path again and again. This trip to work was longer than her walk to Dodge Grocers, she noticed. She came to the bedlam of her apartment, neighbors and fellow workers scattered. They hoped for anything but another dead end, another wall, another failure.

A car was parked on the side of the road outside her apartment, and against the brick building leaned Isaac, Renato's brother. He surveyed her in confusion until she obviously noticed him.

"Heather!" he said and stared at her. Heather threw her arms around him. "Let's go," he said. "You look like hell."

30

The Way of Metal Steps

*H*eather panted deeply in excitement and shouted nothing coherent in joy. She leaped up the metal steps to Mae. Benny and Sylvia were in the apartment. Heather paused in noticeable shock.

"You owe us money!" Benny pointed his finger at her.

"Mae," Heather started and felt courageous ignoring him. Mae had not been awake long. "Come with me," Heather said. Mae followed her sister down the steps and around an opposite corner from Isaac's car.

"Mae," Heather stopped her and cupped her shoulders. "Isaac is here! Renato's brother!" Heather placed a finger over her lips for Mae to stay quiet. "He's here to take us to Savannah, you and me, Mae." Mae looked confused and stared at Heather. "Mae, let's go be happy. Please let me show you."

"I'm ready," Mae answered with no emotion, no caution.

"Okay, do you want to grab your suitcase? Say bye to

Momma?"

"No, can we just go?"

"Just leave everything?"

"Everything? What the hell do we have, Heather?"

Heather paused and answered, "Everything." She directed Mae to Isaac who had his arms opened but a sad look. Heather dashed back up the stairs and grabbed her suitcase. She began placing everything inside: Sylvia's shoes, cigarettes, and clothes. Sylvia and Benny walked out of the back room.

"What are you doing?" Sylvia asked.

"No, Momma, you don't understand," Heather responded in exasperation. "There's a woman down the street, and- and she said she'd give us money, you know, for some of our stuff. I'll bring back what she doesn't buy." Heather tried to place a calm intonation in her words and speak with authoritative lies that her mother nurtured her with, but she couldn't. Benny walked out of the apartment, and Heather stopped packing. She and Sylvia stared at one another.

"I'm leaving, Momma."

Sylvia stared blankly. She sat on the skinny mattress with her knees pointed up. She answered, "Okay, good."

Heather stood with her suitcase in her hand. Sylvia lit a cigarette and looked up at Heather.

"Then go," Sylvia said as she blew out smoke. "Why are you still standing there? What do want, a hug? Go."

Heather wanted to hug her mother, but she stood still a moment more until Sylvia ambled to the back room. *Why did she go back there? Maybe she was crying!*

"Momma?"

Sylvia didn't answer.

"I guess I love you, Momma," Heather stated. She heard her mother laugh.

Heather walked out onto the metal steps descending to the pavement of Atlanta. She noticed the metal screeches and rubbing with each step. She heard her mother ask something at a volume indicating she thought Heather was still close to her. Heather kept walking with a suitcase in her hand and her purse over her shoulder. Some tears fell. Some anguish surfaced.

Mae was already in the backseat of the car, waiting. After placing her luggage in the back with Mae, Heather settled in the front beside Isaac. They pulled away. Heather turned to see Mae gazing at the second-floor apartment door. Mae then met eyes with Heather. Mae had aged, Heather could see it. Heather turned around and watched her daily walk to the Griffins happen in a fast motion. The Griffin children wouldn't be awakened by her in the morning.

She, Isaac, and Mae traveled south. They drove between endless rows of crops down a straight unending road. Heather saw the piano keys in the fields, but she didn't feel like singing.

31

The Jagged Course

The drive lulled Heather and Mae to sleep. Heather awoke feeling rested, as if she had slept for days.

"Are we in Savannah?" she asked. The view didn't look like Georgia anymore, not the Georgia she first saw at the motel. The land was wide, and space was everywhere. Fields lay out in such a stretch that reminded her of home.

"Close," answered Isaac.

The thought struck her: "Are we back in Illinois?" She was horrified.

"Heather, we're practically in Savannah, Doll. See the palm trees?" Palm trees were in patches along the road, and she thought of her father.

They drove for a while in silence.

Heather wondered if Isaac missed his brother. Isaac was

four years older than Renato. He came to visit Renato a few times in Sterling when Isaac did scotch business in Chicago or Pittsburgh.

"Is this the car Renato said was his?" Heather asked.

"He said this car was his?" Isaac lightened his expression. "Sounds like Renato."

"He was missing it back in Illinois."

"Yeah, if I'd shown up, all this would've never happened."

"I'm sorry," Heather stared out the front windshield.

"I'm sorry, too, Heather."

Mae stirred awake. "How much longer, Isaac?"

"Real soon, Mae."

"Isaac, is Savannah like Atlanta?" Mae leaned her head up to talk.

"Not really. I don't think so."

"Good," Mae responded and sat back. Isaac chuckled, and Heather saw a vestige of Renato's mannerisms in the laugh lines on Isaac's face.

Heather didn't cry. Mae asked several questions about Savannah, like were giraffes freely roaming, would they see sharks, or pirates. She asked whether or not Savannah still had slaves and would she and Heather be forced to pick cotton. Isaac kept a smile and enjoyed the entertainment by Mae.

"Mae, I don't know. They have trees that hold onto a moss that's gray and drapes off the trees. That's what Renato told me," Heather answered her. Soon after speaking of them, they saw the live oak trees with massive branches dangling gray long tufts of moss, hanging like thin spiral roots that refused to be underground and unseen.

They arrived in Savannah; the tired day was slowly giving a blue light to the air.

Heather knew the live oak trees and the Spanish moss pulled out and held onto dreams and memories. When she saw one, she thought of her Daddy and of Renato. The trees were mighty and beautiful. Isaac drove under a tunnel of long branches that draped down the moss, twinkling sunlight in small spots, like it was the way of nature's dance.

Isaac pulled into a long driveway in front of a long, one-story house. The air smelled crisp and profuse with cypress sap and salt. Isaac carried the suitcase, and Heather and Mae followed him to the front door. A golden air sprinkled the sky.

"Where are we?" Heather asked.

"My home," he answered. Renato's family.

Mae and Heather were greeted as if the Reyes-Sanchez family had been waiting for them. Many people were in the house. They gathered around Mae and Heather offering tight hugs and long faces with the repeated phrase, "I'm sorry." They knew Heather and Mae lost Hugh and were sad, but Heather refused to cry. A woman with gray hair came into the large living room and stared at Heather and Mae with her arms opened, walking straight to them.

"Mis hijas!" she spoke with a strong Latin accent, "Hugh's girls, ah! I love you. I love you!" She kissed them both on their cheeks and softly let her fingers greet the girls' untamed hair. "I am so glad you are finally here! You will stay here, no? With me."

"Mama Rey?" Heather took a guess. Heather guessed her to be Renato's mother. The lady opened her mouth in surprise and delight and placed her hands down on the lap of her apron.

"That's what Hugh called me! You hear him speak of me, yes?" She smiled in gratitude at Heather and Mae and led them to the kitchen to have a seat. "Your Papa was so good to my sons," she gave them each a glass of water and continued, "Isaac and Renato thought he was so wonderful. And your grandfather, oh!" She looked at Mae, "I have so many wonderful stories to tell you!"

"I have so many stories to tell you, too, Mama Rey," Mae responded, "It's been hell," she spoke regally of her hardships, which amused Heather. She was regaining her intensity. "Mama Rey, can you do my hair? It's getting bigger and bigger. I don't know what's happening to my hair!' Mae wrinkled her face and played with the frizz on her head. Mama Rey laughed.

"They call it hu-mi-di-ty!" She laughed some more. Mae and Heather stared in admiration. Heather looked at Mae for a moment and glanced behind her at the sliding glass doors.

Heather saw eternity. She stood up, completely wrapped in awe. The land stretched with long grass that waved at her, and then ended in flat never-ending water, lying in a twinkle. Mae must have noticed Heather's shock; she looked out and gasped.

"Heather! What are we looking at?"

They walked slowly toward the window. Mama Rey opened the door for them. Mae and Heather walked out with their eyes wide open, afraid to blink and miss any of it. They walked through the soft ground of short grass. Heather took off her shoes to feel it. She could see the black dirt backdropping the soft faded green sprouts. A dock reached out far past the end of the grassy area. They stepped onto the dock and walked until the marsh lay on both sides of them. They walked to the very end of the dock. The water's surface wrinkled in black and dark blue. Heather looked out at the view. It welcomed her to its world, its normal. It kept on doing what it did every day. *How could Renato have left something so beautiful?*

A car drove and parked in the driveway. Heather turned to see, although it was quite a distance from her, and the setting sun blinded her ability to see much. Two men got out of the car. They spoke for a moment, and one of the men began walking through the grass towards the dock.

"Heather, --" Mae started.

The man continued walking, and all Heather could see was his silhouette. As he walked, he rolled up his sleeves.

"Yes, that's— . . . Wait," Mae thought aloud.

The man finally came down enough for them to see him taking off his hat. Renato? This was baffling. Heather was too deep in disbelief to think it could be him, but it was! Heather screamed in delight. Renato walked towards them.

"Renato!" Mae screamed and ran towards him, hugging him tightly. Renato laughed and hugged her back. She wouldn't let go for a long time, so Renato didn't either. Heather walked to him considering he was tied up in Mae's arms. He stared at Heather. Heather returned the stare wide-eyed and panting with excitement. Perhaps he looked differently in Savannah than in everywhere else they had been. His face was peaceful.

"Mae, I love you, but let me hug your sister," Renato's

voice was golden, angelic.

Heather buried her face in his neck as they embraced. After a worthy hug, he took Heather's hand and offered his other hand to Mae. They walked back to the edge of the dock and sat. Mae and Heather leaned in on his chest and shoulders and neck, similar to the evening in the back of the Hawks' truck. But now, they were as far south as Heather wanted to be. A smile rested on their faces.

"This is so nice. You grew up here?" Heather asked.

"Yeah, this is home."

"Have you stepped in that long grass, Ren?" Mae asked.

"Marsh, Mae. It's called marsh. And yes. I had to. I worked in it."

Mae looked confused.

Renato told them, "This is where Isaac and I slithered all through the marsh, running liquor . . . in and out of Georgia and up and down the states. . . It's also where Papa — did you meet him?" They couldn't remember. "Well, you will. This is around the place where Papa first stepped on American land. And he didn't go any further. I, though— I made my last delivery to Chicago and fell in love with the Randolph family."

"So, . . . this is where Daddy lived. Did he look out at this view, too? On this dock?" Heather asked.

"Yeah, he did. All the time."

Renato turned to Mae and said, "Maybe when it's warmer, you and I can swim here."

"I don't think so. There are sharks."

"No, there's not, crazy," he answered, "Maybe some alligators, . . .

"What?"

"Oh, and some manatees. They're bigger than a car, Mae. And a buncha crabs. They got these sharp claws," he joked with Mae and held out his hand to pinch Mae.

"You lie," Mae answered. For quite a while, they bantered, which was fine with Heather. She enjoyed staring at the view. Renato turned to look at her and smiled.

"It's so beautiful," Heather said to break the silence.

He continued to stare at her and answered, "Quite beautiful indeed." His peaceful eyes were more loving than the placid eyes that caused ladies to jitter their knees.

Heather returned with serious information, "Momma's friend Benny said you were dead."

"Bow-tie Man? What a guy, huh? I knew he shouldn't have been wearing a bow tie," Renato joked.

Renato sat quietly for a moment and replied, "Benny was told so. He was told I was dead. I know. I hate that it got back to you."

"Well, it did," Heather said. Renato wrapped an arm around her with assurance. Mae soon became restless and started off the dock to go inside. She was curious once Renato told her Mama Rey had decorated a bedroom just for her.

Renato kept his arm around Heather, and Heather enjoyed his clean smell. He narrowed his eyes out at the ocean. The sky was dimming a dark turquoise. He looked at Heather like he wanted to say something, then he reached into his jacket. On each side he pulled out two shot glasses and a flask. "Did I ever tell you about the time that I first noticed you weren't a little girl anymore?" Heather's curiosity perked.

"I was at the square with Mr. Groches, and I see a beautiful woman walking on the other side of the courthouse. I asked Groches, 'Who is that?' He laughed at me for not recognizing you. I couldn't believe it. You were a girl the day before, and then — this was about a year ago -- I saw you differently."

"You treated me like a girl," Heather answered.

"Not true. I liked having fun with you, and Hugh noticed that I noticed you. I stayed in Sterling because I didn't want to leave you." He handed her a shot, and they shared a toast.

"You and Mae can make new lives here. We can. You're family now. Mama Rey wouldn't have it any other way. We'll make our new lives here, if that's fine with you. There's Prohibition; and then there's the Depression, but you know what? The Reyes-Sanchez family is bigger than both."

Bullfrogs bellowed in full chorus; dark shadows of birds invariably flew over them with loud songs. The air was the same temperature as her skin; it was a part of her skin as if they meshed. Heather fit within Savannah, and she knew she belonged here. She hoped Savannah knew it, too.

"Ren, I'm really here."

"Congratulations." He held up a second shot before he downed it.

"Will Georgia like me?"

"I'll kill 'em if they don't."

"Ren."

"You're right. . . Mae will kill them," Renato laughed.

"We make a mess everywhere we go."

"No worries here. Nothing's gonna change."

"So, . . . We'll still make messes?" she jested. Renato

laughed with her.

Heather was too timid to take a chance to kiss his scotch-glazed lips. She hoped he forgave her for the absent kiss at the jail. She looked out at the marsh; a world of peace stretched to a greater world she couldn't see. The platinum moon's reflection zigzagged through the blackness of pools that claimed homes amidst the marsh. A jagged course, yet moonlit. She knew something about both types of paths.

Renato took Heather's hand and relaxed for a moment with a smile. A breeze enveloped their bodies on the dock, rebuilding their dreams. Her Savannah lover may have been a girlish dream, but a woman can have dreams, too.

I hope you enjoyed this story! Please take a few moments to post a review on Amazon.

www.ingramcontent.com/pod-product-compliance
Lightning Source LLC
Chambersburg PA
CBHW020422110726
47899CB00006B/2093